Island Voices
A collection of Caribbean short stories

CARIBBEAN CONTEMPORARY CLASSICS

Hachette UK's policy is to use papers that are natural, renewable and recyclable products and made from wood grown in well-managed forests and other controlled sources. The logging and manufacturing processes are expected to conform to the environmental regulations of the country of origin.

To order, please visit www.hoddereducation.com or contact Customer Service at education@hachette.co.uk / +44 (0)1235 827827.

© Akhim Alexis, Claudia Allen-Williams, Sharnna Archat Edmonson, Kathleen A Chaitoo, Sherena Christmas, Jodianna R Clarke, Geon Codd, Nardia J Grant, David Hamilton, Dianne Loton-Franklyn, Otancia Noel, Stephanie Ramlogan, Fabian D Smith, Rosetta Thomas

First published by Hodder Education (a trading division of Hodder & Stoughton Limited) in 2023

An Hachette UK Company

Carmelite House
50 Victoria Embankment
London EC4Y 0DZ

www.hoddereducation.com

The authorised representative in the EEA is Hachette Ireland, 8 Castlecourt Centre, Dublin 15, D15 XTP3, Ireland (email: info@hbgi.ie)

Impression number 10 9 8 7 6 5 4 3 2
Year 2027 2026

All rights reserved. Apart from any use permitted under UK copyright law, no part of this publication may be reproduced or transmitted in any form or by any means, electronic or mechanical, including photocopying and recording, or held within any information storage and retrieval system, without permission in writing from the publisher or under licence from the Copyright Licensing Agency Limited. Further details of such licences (for reprographic reproduction) may be obtained from the Copyright Licensing Agency Limited, www.cla.co.uk

Cover illustration © Gabriella D'Abreau
Map by Barking Dog Art
Typeset in 11/15 pt ITC Caslon Regular
Printed in the UK

A catalogue record for this title is available from the British Library.

ISBN 9781036004149

CONTENTS

Introduction x

Map of the Caribbean x

Raya *Otancia Noel* 6

Yankipon *Fabian D Smith* 13

Six O'clock *Nardia J Grant* 31

My Pink Cocoyea Broom *Sherena Christmas* 42

Escape *Rosetta Thomas* 52

Rent Money *Sharnna Archat Edmondson* 66

One an Drive *Jodianna R Clarke* 76

Mount Sheol Private Hospital *Geon Codd* 87

She Wore Red to the Cremation *Stephanie Ramlogan* 96

Memories of the River *Claudia Allen-Williams* 104

Bush Tea *Akhim Alexis* 111

Heaven Help Us *David Hamilton* 123

Remember Me *Dianne Loton-Franklyn* 138

Creatures in the Ackee Tree *Kathleen A Chaitoo* 147

Meet the authors 159

Also available 164

INTRODUCTION

In 2021 and 2022, we celebrated the launch of Hodder Education's Caribbean Contemporary Classics list and embarked on a mission to unearth the untapped literary talent of the Caribbean. This volume stands as a testament to that mission, presenting a compilation of winning entries that resonate with the islands' vibrant rhythms and diverse voices.

These stories are not just tales; they reflect the Caribbean's society, history and vibrant culture. They showcase the Caribbean dynamic in an engaging and transformative way, with writers masterfully weaving English and French Creoles into captivating dialogues.

Dive into these pages and witness the promising growth of these writers. Embrace these new stories and be inspired to explore more works by these prize-winning authors.

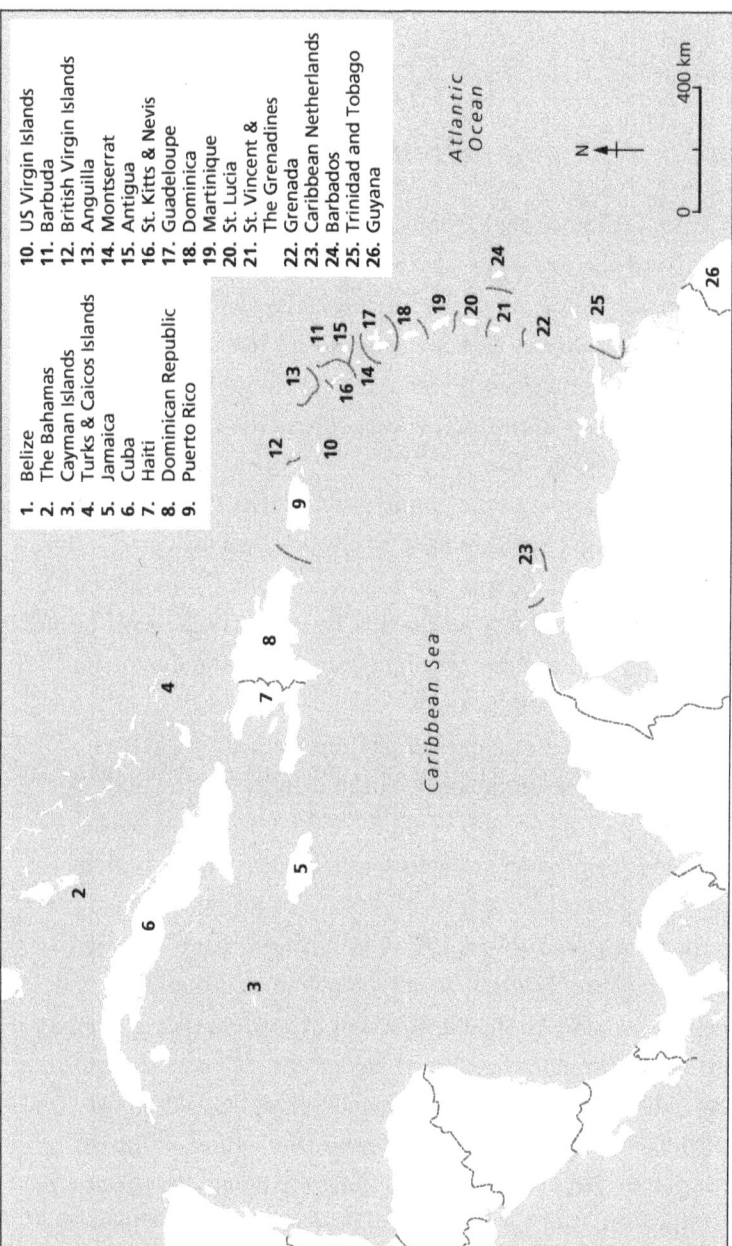

RAYA
Otancia Noel

IT WAS THE hour that the dead man birds' calls could be heard and she waited to hear the shrill piercing sound of the whistle, an indication of the time to leave. Her grandparents were asleep upstairs and downstairs with her were her four siblings. The grandparents' son, the revolutionist, was in jail and her mother in the city, taking care of his needs. But life wasn't always like that …

Life was serene in the countryside of Irie. Mother was always at home, Pa and Ma were usually on the estate across the river. And father? Well, he was never at home; only God knows what he was doing. Mother thought that he was a truck driver or maxi-taxi driver at that time. When he was not on the job, he was in town with the Ismal Party.

Ten-year-old Raya and her siblings walked to and from school with other children from the neighbourhood, kicking crapaud, picking gru gru bef and paddu, ringing the house bells and running off and harassing the dogs and cats along the way. Being the eldest grandchild of the renowned estate owner in the village, she always had to be a little less adventurous than the other children, because some macco would see and then Ma would give them a good cut arse when they got home. She always thought that the villagers were telepathic. How else could they see, hear and know everything and report to Ma before the children could even think about doing the things? So, after school she did not stray much like the other children; she and her siblings went home and basically played the afternoon away on their grandparents' estate. There was always something to do on the estate besides the things that Ma wanted them to do that never got done. The estate was like an enchanted forest with acres of flowers like orchids and anthuriums; fields of fruit trees; cocoa and coffee fields; Ma's variety of herbs and spices; massive groves of bamboo lining the river bank; teak, palm trees and the majestic towering cypress and silk cotton trees scattered across the land. Nestled inside this forest were her grandparents' two-storey four-bedroom concrete house and 'the old house' with its large porcelain ancient-looking bathtub which she and all her siblings fitted into quite comfortably. This was the two-bedroom wooden house where her father and his nine siblings had grown up.

Some days they had a treasure hunt, other days a picnic. They climbed the pommerac and mango trees. They fished in the river or just fed the caimans – well, the argument was always about 'it's an alligator, no, we only have caiman', her older brother Raul, the serious one, usually insisted. Sometimes, they caught small river crabs and boiled them in milk pans on the river bank. They never ate these but whenever their English or Yankee cousins visited, they would usually offer them this traditional delicacy, assuring them that they ate this all the time.

Of course, when Ma caught them they had to help feed the chickens, the ducks, the pigs; grind spices and help to make the fruit preserves from plum, mango, sour cherry or whatever fruit was in season. And they had to listen to Ma's stories about how life was easy for them, how hard it was 'back in the days in Grenada' when Ma was a little girl getting up 'before cock crow' to do all the work on the cocoa estate then walking for miles barefooted through the estate and 'crossing the river' to go to school. Ma would then launch an attack on 'nowadays children', who she swore were spawns of the devil.

'No respect, no manners, Lord Jesus!' Ma would say as she rocked back and forth while doing whatever odd job she would be doing at the time. You couldn't even think about bringing one of those spawns into the estate yard, Ma would say. 'Stick to yourself. Is four ah allyuh. That is enough, and don't ask the neighbour (who was a good walk away) for some salt even. Don't take anything from anybody in school or otherwise. Forget allyuh father and he religious nonsense.'

These were some of Ma's life lessons that she chanted to us on what seemed like an hourly basis.

But let me tell you about Ma. She was a strong woman, wise and proud. She worked very hard to achieve all that she had on the little island of Irie, which she had come to at the age of seventeen and worked first as a servant. Then she married Pa who came from Grenada a year after her. Pa, on the other hand, the product of a mulatto mother and white father, was the typical laid back womaniser and socialite, but he did his part. Ma kept him in line. Pa couldn't work as long or as hard as Ma, and he often lamented about 'the hot sun on my white skin' but the grandkids usually clung to Pa. He was 'our salt fish grandpa', who would let us get away with murder. Ma sometimes left the house while they were still dreaming, with her cutlass, a flask of coffee and a piece of bake. She came back when they were dragging in from school, with a feed bag of yam on her back and another bag on her head with plantain or some other produce from the land.

Ma's significance, sacrifice and strength were only recognised by Raya and her siblings years later, when they were adults and decided to go to the fields on their own. That morning they prepared themselves, well-armed and dressed for the part in all their safety gear for gardening. Well, they came home with one piece of yam about the length of a six-month-old baby's arm and bites from an army of ants and all other insects that they couldn't name. Now, mind you, this was after they spent the entire day digging, cutting and even drilling for yam, eddoes and dasheen. The next day they couldn't even get out of bed due to fever and allergies. Her brother Saud looked like a potato that was left in the oven for too long and he had to walk around for the next four days looking like a ghost covered in calamine lotion, since he also suffered from Pa's white skin disease. Imagine, Ma did all that work on her own and collectively they couldn't achieve what she did single handedly in one day.

The serenity of life in the countryside was broken a few days after Raya's twelfth birthday in August of 1987. The prodigal son, who had begun to spend even more time with the Ismal Party over the past year, had finally convinced his wife to leave the estate with their kids for the greater cause in the city.

Ma was distraught. 'Let him go by heself,' she said to Mother. 'Don't leave here with meh grandchildren to go between all them mad people.'

But love prevailed and life went on to teach them a lesson that left a scar on the skin's surface but an open wound beneath that ran deep within the network of blood capillaries and nerve endings in their family.

Life in the big city of Port-de-Irie was very different for Raya and her siblings. For one, there was no great expanse of land to frolic in but she and her siblings made do with the dunks and jamon trees on the compound and the big drain at the back of the compound with the mangroves that stood at the far southern end. They lived community-style with about 20 other families, in an apartment complex on the eastern side. There were two sets of communal bathroom and toilet facilities for everyone on the compound, of course with the exception of Jacob himself, who had his own bathroom facilities within his large apartment.

Island Voices

Mother now followed the prodigal son around and became an active member of the Party, so Raya was now the house manager. There was a school on the compound and a small grocery. Most times they did not venture outside of the compound yard. Raya and her siblings spent countless days at home alone or just running around the compound with the other children after school. There were some structured activities like a karate class, a baking class for women, an educational class and a religious class. The compound was life and life was the compound. School was there, everyone was there, and there was an increasing number of ex-gang members, nobodies and homebodies, coming and going, living and passing through daily, monthly, yearly.

And over the next three years Ma's voice travelled long and far. During those years she lamented about the condition of her grandchildren whenever they came home for holidays, sometimes with ringworms in their heads, or with bad manners. Raul was getting even more serious and bringing 'all kinda stupid book with gun and knife in the place.'

Ma wanted to know exactly what was going on 'up in that place in town'. Her lamentations fell into the river and swam away with the tide. And as Ma predicted, 'who doh hear does feel'. The revolution came exactly three years after they had left the countryside. Raul was killed in action and the prodigal son was jailed.

Life moved fifteen-year-old Raya, Mother and her siblings back to the countryside. This was after they had spent two months in a 'shelter' for the wives and children of the revolutionists. It was like coming into a whole new world again. Life as it stood already held challenges for Raya, being on the brink of womanhood, and now it was even more challenging after the bloody revolution. It was not as easy as one might think to make the necessary adjustment into public school and mainstream society, especially with the whole revolutionary thing hanging like a black cloud over her head.

People were curious about her and her family after this episode in their lives. Everyone wanted to know what happened: as if she was in the city totting a gun and killing people, rather than cowering under her bed when the soldiers came and took her family and the other women and children from the compound while her father and his gang were fighting for the cause. She just remembers that it was a Friday like any other Friday. There was the midday religious sermon, then most of the men got into a few maxis that were on the compound. They were going to their usual Friday gathering in the square or so she and many others thought. But by the time all the birds were finding their nest and the television in the hall was turned on for the usual Friday evening movie, they saw on the screen Jacob flanked by two men – one who looked quite a lot like Raul – in army gear with guns.

Jacob's now famous words resonated across the country, 'The country is now under siege. Please keep calm and follow the orders of our troops. I repeat, please keep calm and follow the orders of our troops,' and the rest was history.

After this, by nightfall, the army swooped down on the compound firing their guns and loaded everyone into buses taking them to the shelter. When they were finally released from the shelter, Raya even had her own police entourage to and from school. Soldiers and police raided her home constantly and life was chaotic. And she often wondered what the point was, seeing that Father was already locked away and Raul, her only brother, was dead. Pa was a ghost after the revolution and Ma, well she was just Ma.

Anyhow, bit by bit Raya got back into society. She made friends, had a boyfriend, wore the latest fashion and did all the other trivial things teenagers did. But then there was another challenge rearing its head. She and Mother now had varying views and ideas on life, on religion, and on the do's and don'ts. Mother, who was not home most times, practically handed the helm of motherhood to Ma and more so to Raya, in order to take care of Father and his band of 'for the cause' brothers. Raya's responsibilities were a bit too much for a teenager who just wanted to do normal teenage things like wear jeans, go to a friend's house or to a birthday party. Mother disagreed with everything Raya wanted to do. Ma agreed and sometimes disagreed, but Ma was willing to find a common ground. Since, as Ma put it, 'She is old enough and if she don't want to be in allyuh thing then leave she.' Mother was not putting up with that so whenever she was around it was 'do as I say'. Raya began to resent Mother because of the fact that Mother had followed Father to town and he got them into the mess that they had been in, then Mother brought them back to a world that Raya had been alienated from. Raya saw herself as struggling to find her place in this world and not wanting to be in Mother's and Father's world. Now Mother wanted to control her, while not being there to support her through the struggles.

This new dilemma led Raya to make a decision.

She stands on the edge of the darkness clutching her bag pack. It is the hour that the dead man birds' calls can be heard and she waits to hear the shrill piercing sound of the whistle, an indication of the time to leave. Her grandparents are asleep upstairs. Downstairs with her are her four siblings. She looks back at her sleeping siblings. She knows that she will miss them dearly, but as Raul always said, 'The wind always blows change.' The shadows of ghosts from the past taunt her. As the whistle blows, she wipes the drops from her eyes and steps out.

YANKIPON

Fabian D Smith

RUMOURS OF WAR were on every lip from Seville to the Guanaboa Forests. From each of them, every word of the rumour, the same:

> *The English brave the Atlantic aboard HMS King Charles, a hulking brute of a warship. Its anatomy of oak, hosting no less than 120 pieces of artillery; its decks, enough red coats to deluge the island.*

Juan never conflated rumours with truth. In any case, his mind was occupied with dreams that robbed him of sleep, and the one who could provide him answers.

'Do your dreams fill you with dread? Do you despair?'

The witch was a nocturnal creature of the wood. She came with the rising of the moon, and like any other being, had a purpose, a design. She assumed too much.

Juan de Bolas of the Wayward Windward Maroons was never one to despair. From Yallahs in the east to Seville in the north, the Maroons and Spaniards had seen him wield a machete in the field. They knew he was fearless.

'I told you, woman. I was travelling on a road made of light. It was leading me into the sky.'

'What then?'

'Suddenly, the road vanishes. I am standing upon the earth … I see it. A peculiar rose. A green rose. It blooms from a stone-paved path. All else is barren, save for that rose.'

The old woman was draped in a cloak resembling a tattered curtain. Beneath it, her wrinkled face changed into a scowl. Had he soured her mood? Was she unbothered?

'Do you have the answer to my dream or not, old woman?'

'The question, Young Juan ... is do you?'

The old woman was by no means noble company. After all, the Spanish called her Bruja (witch). A fitting title. The woman knew things no man or woman should know, yet shared so little of what she knew. *Perhaps she knows very little.*

All the while, Juan's machete lay across his lap, a playful finger charting the length of the blade. Juan was never far from his machete at any given time.

'You will come into power, Juan,' she proclaimed. 'You will come to know power and hubris with it. Like all proud men, that pride shall leave you as will your glory. But your deeds shall know longevity.'

'Explain.'

'Did I not explain to you just now, boy?'

'Woman,' Juan was getting loud. He glanced around at the tents surrounding them. Within them lie other members of the Wayward Maroons resting for a busy and perilous day ahead. Juan should do the same, yet here he was arguing with a witch.

The old woman raised a shrivelled hand and placed it about her ear as she leaned into the bushes. 'Do you hear that?' She was frantic. Her smile revealed a myriad of missing teeth. 'The bushes speak, Juan. They speak your name, your glory... your tragedy.'

Juan felt anger rising in him. He collected himself and decided to return to his tent. There was much to do come the morning; it was best he had a clear head. Chief Esteban de Milla would be meeting with the Spanish General, Don Javier de Ysasi, to discuss important matters about the future of the Maroons, the future of Jamaica.

Juan would not miss the meeting if his life depended on it. He rose to his feet, gave the old woman a look of disdain, then retreated to his tent.

***

When the night was darkest, he dreamt of Gabriella. He remembered her as he had known her: beautiful and free. Then the image of her changed, her tunic clothes sullied and ripped, and she was swallowed by a potent blackness; there was nothing left but her terrible visage, hanging in the empty darkness, beaten and chequered by ghastly wounds.

'Don't,' her voice wept, echoed by the harrowing screams of a hundred men and women. 'Don't look back!'

Juan had seen men fall to the machete more times than he could count, yet her tear-streaked face alone put fear in his heart. A part of him feared that he might live here, in this madness, forever. But then he was ripped out of his dream, violent hands dragging him from the never-ending depths of a lonely grave.

***

Morning came, and Juan was the last to wake. Eyes open, he reached over for his machete. He then rose from the bed, strapped it to his waist, his weapon fitting nicely into his goatskin belt. He peeled the flaps of the tent open. The sun met his eyes, a harsh greeting. He meant to fetch some water to wash himself, but already it was too late. The Wayward Maroons were lined up, being addressed by the Chief.

Juan fell in beside his comrades: Ricardo to his left, Camilo his right, both snickering as he joined them. No doubt, there had been jokes about him oversleeping on such a morning.

Esteban did not address him. The Chief had more pressing matters on his mind. 'As you know, this is the day we meet with Don Javier de Ysasi, the Spanish General. In the past, we have had many skirmishes against him and his men. I know some of you hate him still, while others would prefer we focus our strengths ... elsewhere.'

Juan bristled.

'I ask that we put these issues aside until we have rid ourselves of our English foe.'

Camilo, who stood to Juan's right, was a large, stocky Maroon. His arms were like great logs, and his powerful legs and broad chest made him an imposing figure. Camilo was something of a gentle giant. He laid a consoling hand on Juan's shoulder.

Ricardo was the opposite of Camilo. Small in stature. Big in temper. He slapped a consoling, slightly more aggressive hand on Juan's other shoulder.

'We will save them, Juan,' said Esteban. 'We will travel north and save Gabriella, and the others. I promise.'

'By then, they will have been murdered,' said Juan. 'Or beaten and tortured out of their minds. We know what happens to Blacks on a plantation; that is why our people refused to become slaves. That is why we fight.'

The Maroons began to murmur among themselves.

'I take your meaning, Juan,' Esteban allowed. 'But we must plan wisely and decide our next move. It grieves me deeply that your people, born free, have been taken into slavery. Carlo Perez de Leon has committed a most shocking crime. And he will pay. But first, we must tend to the English at our door.'

Esteban threw his gaze upon the young Maroon faces all around him. 'Now is not the time for us to despair. We must depart from Guanaboa and hold counsel with de Ysasi and his men in Withywood. We must seal this peace to put an end to the conflict.'

'Why not rid ourselves of the Spanish? Unite with the English?' Ricardo joked.

The Maroons seemed to hold their breath. Esteban was a compassionate leader. Kind-hearted. Strong. Ruthless if necessary. Above all else, he did not tolerate insolence.

The Chief already stood close to seven feet tall, but after Ricardo's comment, he appeared to grow five inches taller. His arms clamped with gold bracelets, right hand clutching his musket, Esteban towered over Ricardo. 'I care little for both Spanish and English,' the Chief admitted. 'But should we turn from our potential Spanish alliances, Maroons from here to Yallahs will have our heads. Many still harbour grudges and may be looking to spring a surprise attack as we speak. Is it your fancy to leave this world in a grizzly ambush?'

Esteban stared down into the eyes of his young warrior.

Ricardo met his glare. 'It is not, Chieftain.'

'Then we are of a mind.'

***

In under an hour, the Maroons had pulled down their tents and were set to journey into Withywood. The morning air remained crisp; the leaves of the surrounding trees glistened with dew. From the depths of the bushes came a hundred songs of birds and insects.

Juan drank it all in. He turned to join the others when he noticed, in the bushes, flies huddled excitedly: a black cloud with a million commingled, moving parts. He approached to find the source of their amusement, and encountered an affront to his nostrils, the stink of death and rot. Between the trees lay the carcass of what had been a ferocious boar, its tusks erected like the mighty spears of a warrior, fallen in battle.

The council between the Wayward Maroons and de Ysasi concluded with a handshake in a tavern in Withywood. The agreement was followed by a solemn silence. It was decided: Together, they would smite the English.

General de Ysasi was kind enough to loan the Wayward Maroons horses. Fifteen men rode while the bulk of Esteban's force trotted on foot; a gaggle of scouts pushed ahead to ensure the path wasn't perilous.

As they took narrow paths into the thick bushes, Ricardo, atop his horse, fell in beside them. They were discussing the meeting with de Ysasi.

'Did that Spaniard really ask if we knew how to ride horses?' he said, aghast.

'These white men continue to underestimate us,' said Camilo.

'As we continue to underestimate them,' Juan offered. 'I care little for this Spanish General. I mean only to be rid of the English. Then I shall ride north to the de Leon Plantation, with or without the help of our Chieftain.'

Silence.

Camilo watched his friend for a long moment. 'Gabriella was a good girl, Juan. She was sweet and kind.'

'*Was?*' Juan's blood began to boil. Camilo spoke as though Gabriella was dead already.

'Consider that she is no longer of this world,' said Camilo. The clopping of hooves filled the gaps of silence in their exchange. 'You killed Carlos de Leon's right-hand man. This is something the Spaniard will not soon forget.'

Juan bristled and spoke no more. He thought only of Gabriella, how they had grown together and loved each other. How they retreated to the village in Mountain Top and danced to the drums as they feasted in the heart of the night. How she told him of Madrid and the world of which their parents often spoke.

Among Maroons, the blood of Africa ran deep as a silent river. Their children sprang from bloodlines, originating from as far as Sudan. Others traced their roots to the Blacks who occupied Spain in days of old. Forever banished, they were scattered across Europe and the unknown world. He recalled he Spanish Inquisition, the Spaniard faith that influenced him to this day. It was a concept foreign to most Maroons, a topic better avoided.

Suddenly, Esteban froze atop his horse. The Maroons on foot and horseback did the same. The bushes were thick about them, but in the silence, Juan sensed something rustling in its depths. Something wicked and violent that loved them not. *The enemy is here.*

The song of a bird flitted through the bushes. It travelled between the trees, the wood and the plants. It was a warning. Juan de Bolas, as well as his comrades, knew this song came not from the birds, but from the scouts who had set out ahead of them to warn of impending danger.

That danger has come.

The Eastern Militia came from the bushes, clutching knives and machetes and crying for their gods. In a brilliant clash, they met; blade biting through flesh as easily as if it were a piece of bread.

Ricardo and Camilo rode with Juan.

The woods were now a melting pot of shouts and blades and was enough to make a man dizzy. The singing of blades a shrill song, deafening to the ears; but he had known it by heart by the time he was thirteen.

On hind legs, his horse neighed madly as enemies swarmed them like insects. Juan fiercely wielded his machete at every turn.

Blade met shoulder, skull and forearm, and the enemy wailed and went reeling into their ranks. A short victory, for

Juan knew they would not rest until they had taken him from atop his horse.

And he was right. A pack of younglings coalesced and pushed towards him like a wave, riding hard over the forest bed.

He knew what they were doing but the wave was too fast and too vicious, and the crash had been sudden. The wave consumed man and horse and they tumbled to the earth. He remembered only the taste of dirt, a faint but unmistakable ringing in his ears.

It took him a second to return to his senses, and he flew to his feet when he did. Juan planted his blade in the flesh of an enemy and then another. Blood splattered upon his face but he didn't care; a part of him revelled in the savagery.

It wouldn't last. The veil of invincibility was fleeting. He found that the strength of his limbs was waning: a mountain fire quelled by hazardous rain. Then he saw him. Amid the chaos as Maroon fought Maroon, a cloaked stranger shifted through the sea of blades.

'Yankipon!' a man cried.

'The ancestors are with us!' cried another. 'Cut them down! Yankipon is with us!'

Their cries met the heavens like thunder.

Yankipon!

Yankipon!

Yankipon!

Juan watched another enemy collapse to his death as Esteban's mountainous frame appeared in the distance. His horse, too, was dead, but his spirit was very much alive as he chopped men to death and shot them to pieces, his machete and musket possessed by a spirit of war.

Then it happened.

Upon turning on his heel, Esteban took a machete to the neck. He fell hard. The collapse of his body was such that he was clearly dead.

Juan was distracted for no more than a second before an enemy tried to capitalise with a swift stroke of their blade. Camilo appeared between them as if it were magic and seized the enemy by the throat. Help the Chief!

Juan knew it was too late. However, his feet moved without his permission, taking him closer to the one who had killed Esteban. Foe men threw themselves in front of him in an attempt to block his path, only to be struck by what seemed to be lightning; they were instead arrows fired from a ruthless bow. If Ricardo were in front of Juan at the moment, he would have hugged the fool for saving his life – but there was no time.

Juan's problems were only beginning. The one who killed Esteban was a legend whose reputation did him a disservice: He was as tall as the Chief, strong as a bear, and preferred using two machetes to one. The English visited in recent years and had faced him in battle.

The big man was a ferocious sight. Juan fought hard to subdue his fear. His life streamed before him in the final moment, a chain of memories: he was a child, then a teen, then a warrior, each lasting a second longer than time.

The first was of his father. Juan sat on his shoulders, and they sang and laughed in the shade of a tree. The second was on the banks of Rio Minho, under the blue of a sweet summer sky; his heart leapt at her every word, as he stared into the eyes of the only woman he ever loved. Gabriella melted sweetly into his arms. Her lips met his in a feverish kiss and sunlight dappled the face of the river.

The last one appeared, more vivid than the others. They named him 'warrior'; Maroons gathered in anticipation. The

Chief approached and wrapped a goatskin belt about his waist. Pride swelled inside him and tears streaked his face. Head flung back, he cried into the sky.

Then the memories stopped. And there was darkness. And Juan knew that he was dead. But the darkness was fleeting; death was brief. And again, he lived and cried, and fought, chaos unfurling around him like the coils of a snake.

Ricardo worked his bow like a musical instrument, a foe collapsing with every pluck of the string. Camilo roared and raged and barrelled over enemies like a brown bear desperate to protect its young. Then came the machete, swinging sideways to remove the head from his shoulders. Certainly, it would have done so, had it struck its blow.

Like before, Juan's legs moved of their own volition. They stepped to the left; the machete missed by an inch. His legs moved ever so slightly to the right and avoided the other. In their exchange, there was a moment of nothingness, and Juan filled the gap with a swing of his own.

Then it was over. Like a dream, it was over. His machete came away accompanied by the head of the Boar. Juan stood there forever. His breath, heavy. His hands, raw. His entire being ached with the strains of battle. When the enemy fled, he couldn't say; he saw only his comrades encircling him in curious motions. On their lips were the songs of the bushes, emotions felt by the spirit.

Yankipon!

Yankipon!

Ricardo often appeared unfeeling, yet even he seemed close to tears. A rare sight. Juan had never seen him cry.

The hooded one lingered like a spirit of the wood, floating between dancing Maroons. How strange. Juan alone had eyes to see it.

For a moment, confusion struck like a weapon. But like death, it was fleeting, fading into glorious knowledge. The Maroons believed Yankipon guided him to glory. But this favour came not from the gods of the bushes. They were wrong. And yet he dared not voice the revelation. Instead, he rejoiced in the Spirit and the very old promise of eternal life.

Heart weeping. Arms opened. Juan de Bolas exalted.

In the coming days, word spread to all corners of Jamaica of the newly elected leader of the Wayward Maroons. Under Juan de Bolas, they were now called the Black Militia. Word spread of a new contract with de Ysasi, securing the defeat of the English, and the salvation of those enslaved by de Leon.

His strength replenished, Juan was moving north in Guanaboa with more than 220 warriors, strengthened by a portion of de Ysasi's force. In his heart, he hoped his contract with the Spanish would free the one he loved, and – if they were fortunate – secure a future for his island home.

***

'Our scouts are in place. Morale is high among the front liners. I suspect we shall arrive in good time,' said the big man for the five-hundredth time.

The clash with the English was days away and they were making excellent time. Camilo, however, thought it necessary to remind him every so often.

'Thank you, Camilo. Now could you be so kind as to share what it is that troubles you,' said Juan, adjusting slightly the reins of his horse.

'Forgive me, brother. I did not sleep well. Something has caused me a great unease, and to make it worse, I know not what it is.'

Juan fell silent. He, too, felt perturbed. The past night he had dreamt of Gabriella once again: her face floating in the darkness. 'Don't look back ... Don't look back', she had cried throughout the night. To recall her beaten face, her desperate cry, made his heart collapse into his stomach.

His grip on the reins tightened considerably.

Ricardo rode up alongside them. 'This is the place. We should hitch the horses off this path. The trees off this track seem a good place.'

Juan agreed. 'Tell our Spanish friends.'

Ricardo gave him the look. Camilo snickered.

Juan conceded. 'Fine, I will tell them.'

Once the Maroons and Spaniards had hitched their horses, Juan and de Ysasi's second-in-command, Juarez, began discussing strategy. They sat on the side of the path, watching their men populate the main road.

'I agree with this plan,' said Juarez. 'We bait them with fifty of my men to distract them. Your Maroons will then have time to complete their flank ...'

Juarez's voice became a murmur in the back of Juan's mind. He could focus only on the two runaway slaves tearing through nearby bushes, their clothes ripped, their faces bruised and bloodied. They collapsed among the Maroons and Spaniards on the road.

Juan and his men approached them straight away. 'What has happened? Where are you from?' he demanded.

Their story was not one he wanted to hear. The older of the two, a black man with weary eyes, spoke in grave tones.

'We are coming from the de Leon Plantation. We have come to tell you of Carlos and Don Javier, the man called de Ysasi. They plan to destroy you and the Black Militia after your victory over the English.'

The slave claimed that de Ysasi and de Leon intended to parade the broken body of a slave girl to greet Juan as he returned from battle. They would disgrace her, relish in the torture of her flesh before ending the lives of Juan and his men.

'It is a lie!' called Juarez. His voice was trembling.

Why? Juan wondered. *Why would the General do this?*

The younger of the runaways said, 'Carlos and Javier are not merely allies. They are blood. Carlos de Leon is his own cousin.'

Juan tore his eyes from the bloodied slaves before him to look upon Juarez's sweat-covered face. By now, the Spaniard knew: no words spoken from his lips would save him.

***

No Spaniard drew breath at the end of the battle. Juan stood by, observing the road strewn with the bodies of Maroon and Spaniard as he discussed further plans with his clan.

'We have come this far, Juan. What shall we do?' asked Camilo. Ricardo, ever thoughtful, stood by in anticipation.

'De Ysasi will believe we have gone ahead with the plan,' said Juan. 'We must give him no cause to think otherwise. He is unaware of the slaves who escaped and knows nothing of their intention to seek me out. So, I charge you with the mission I had entrusted to de Ysasi. Camilo, you will lead 130 of our Maroons to the de Leon Plantation. They are not well guarded and will not be expecting an attack. Ricardo, you will be responsible for Gabriella. You will take her to Mountain Top when the smoke has cleared.'

Ricardo gave Juan the look.

Juan clapped a hand on his shoulder. 'I need you, my brother. Please, do this for me.'

Ricardo shrugged. Camilo looked worried. 'If we take 130 of the men, how will you fight the English?'

'My mission does not require a great army,' said Juan. 'Truthfully, I would have sent you both to face the English, but …'

His thoughts trailed off. Again, he was in his dreams, dark and foreboding. Gabriella's face swimming in the abyss. *Don't look back …*

'Juan, speak to us,' pleaded Camilo, the gentle giant.

'Fret not, my brothers. When this battle is won, we, the Maroons, shall be the Old Jamaicans. Gather your strength. Prepare to crush de Ysasi and de Leon.'

Juan ascended his horse and called his warriors to join him. 'Ricardo, when Camilo and the others are burning the de Leon Plantation to the ground, look for me in that special place. Together, we shall travel to Mountain Top.'

Juan could not bear to look into the eyes of his comrades as he descended into Spanish Town with twenty of his men in tow. *Don't look back*. Gabriella's voice was that of a ghost, haunting him now as it did his dreams. And yet, it filled him with resolve.

Juan tightened his hands on the hilt of the machete: the one that belonged to the Great Boar of the Wood. Not many knew that in the days of his prime, the Boar was known as the Bane of the English.

The Black Militia fell upon the plantation like sudden rain; an assault which ended with slave owners kneeling on the front lawn chained and pleading for their lives. Slaves were freed in their scores, Maroons pillaged the property, and the Spirit of the Ancestors exalted.

From the outliers of the battle, arrows flew with precision, picking slavers off like the scabs of old wounds. The wood of the bow was smooth and the arrows flew with a hiss that was music to his ears.

Ricardo was no ambassador of violence. It was an option he would sooner avoid, yet his warrior's heart rejoiced with every kill.

At the end of the battle, de Ysasi and de Leon were left to the mercy of Camilo. How unfortunate for them, that the big man had little mercy for slavers. Both were stowed on horses and taken away into the mountains.

The sun had yet to rise when he saw her. Gabriella was limping through the battered doors of the great house, beaten and bruised, a rose in the midst of chaos. Ricardo remembered her well; they had shared a childhood in Mountain Top, after all. Gabriella was brave and kind and clever. She deserved not such a fate. She smiled when he approached her and that gave him pause. He thought by now she would be dead, or at the very least broken. The girl hugged him.

'He knew you were alive,' he said, arms lolling at his sides. *He always knows.*

That's when they saw him: A young warrior bolting across the lawn with urgent news on his lips. News that had come from the newly-elected Chief: 'He has joined the English! Juan de Bolas has joined the English!'

Finally, Ricardo understood. *When this battle is won, we, the Maroons, shall be the Old Jamaicans.*

He and his comrades were almost in place for the decisive attack. They trotted along a cliffside heading for the path to Seville.

The outpost was nestled in the shrubs of the north, where they would rejoin the army, along with Camilo and the other Maroons.

Juan's mind was with Gabriella, his brothers. He wondered if everything had gone according to his plan. That was when it appeared.

Past the gully, there was a plain, a gorgeous stretch of land. It failed to impress as much as the rose that had bloomed in its centre: the rose from his dreams. His distraction did not go unnoticed.

'Chieftain, are you alright?' asked a young warrior named Daniel.

'Yes.'

Silence for a moment. Then Juan looked to his allies. 'Please, go ahead to the camp. I will be there with you shortly.'

The Maroons were visibly concerned.

'Please, trust me.'

Once they were gone, Juan slunk down the cliffside like a large cat. Then through the gully and onto the open plain. He got a better look at the rose: it was large with petals green as spring, sitting in a vibrant bed of grass.

He had gone to one knee, observing it like a child might a new toy, when he noticed the hooded stranger before him. Juan never looked up at the figure. He simply smiled and turned to face them.

Enemy Maroons loomed from the depths of the surrounding bushes. *They've been tracking us all this time.*

'No,' he said aloud. 'They were looking for *me*.'

Juan did not run. Arms open, he recalled the fight in the bushes alongside his brothers. He recalled the protection bestowed upon him. He felt gratitude. The enemy moved closer to cut him down.

'Thou art the resurrection and the life,' he called to the empty sky. 'He who believeth in thee, though he should die, yet shall he live.'

He drew his knife from its goatskin sheath. Then rose to face his enemies one last time.

***

They had been walking for two days, Mountain Top ever within reach. Throughout the journey, Gabriella had spoken little. He never knew her to be quiet but supposed her silence should be expected. The hilly terrain was leading them into the mountain and they came upon a precipice. Below, the whole of Jamaica seemed to spread out before them: sparse villages riding a rich green sea. They stopped to admire the view.

'Worry not,' said Ricardo. 'Juan will have crushed the Spanish. He will be with us soon.'

A gentle breeze swept the path before them. 'Don't you see?' said Gabriella. 'He is already with us.' Her hands caressed the roundness of her belly and for a moment he was speechless. Ricardo cursed himself for not noticing before.

Their eyes met. 'I wanted him to know. But I suppose he does. Does he not?'

'Praise Yankipon.' Ricardo closed his eyes and said a short prayer to the Ancestors and his God.

They started on the path once more, footsteps crunching on leaves.

'Didn't he tell you?' her tone was casual. 'There is one God. And Yankipon is not His name.'

The words were accompanied by a shriek of pain, and he spun to see she had collapsed. Struggling to her feet, she winced against the pain. He darted to her side, helped her to stand.

Together, they watched the lands below them.

'Do you believe there is a future here?' she asked him. 'A Jamaica where our people are truly free?'

'Yes,' he said, and cursed himself for the lie.

Sunlight broke over the trees and towns. The nearest village had stirred awake. Children poured into the streets, and their parents followed. Laughter. Freedom. Ricardo had never seen this outside of a mountain village. It stirred within him an

Island Voices

emotion he could not describe nor understand. Another moment passed and Ricardo thought it didn't matter in the end.

He wiped the tears from his eyes.

SIX O'CLOCK
Nardia J Grant

THE CALAMITY WAS unforgettable. The roaring, crackling, red, yellow and orange flames illuminated that dark summer's night. The smell of the burning house and a strange scent that I could not identify at the time was pungent and asphyxiating, blanketing the entire community like a sheet. It was utter chaos. The calamity was unforgettable.

The men got to work. Running with buckets and buckets of water to douse the flames. They formed water leagues and chains as they battled the merciless flames, but the more they poured, the angrier the flames grew. More people came and more people helped, but man was no match for fire that night. Resistance was futile, but their indomitable spirit never said die.

Above the noise and the chaos, a most harrowing scream rang out from the top floor of the Anderson's mansion.

'Heeeeelllppp! Somebody, heeeelllppp! Pleeeeease!'

I knew that voice anywhere. It was Elizabeth, the fairest of little girls in Buckston Hill, my true and dearest friend. Everybody was shocked to realise that someone was inside. Everyone thought they had gone into Kingston for the weekend, as was their custom. Panic set in and efforts to get inside the house went to fever pitch. They tried to break down the doors and smash the windows, but at every entrance pillars of smoke and raging flames repelled their every attempt.

Elizabeth kept on screaming. The men kept on working. The women kept on praying. The fire kept on raging.

It seemed like an eternity, but within minutes the house was fully engulfed and Elizabeth's screams faded within it. The women pulled their headties and their sweaters to gird their loins and bellowed the most ear piercing wails that I ever heard. The men held their heads in desperation as the sprawling white mansion was reduced to blackened walls and ash right before our eyes. There was nothing else that could be done. We watched it burn until fire had had her fill. Only then did she relent to the water of men. Fire had won.

I stood there, numb.

Then the old bell at the Baptist Church began to toll. Dong! Dong! Dong!

Nobody slept that night. There was sighing, weeping and moaning. Grief overpowered the living and they felt like hell had opened its mouth and devoured their souls.

As first light began peeking over the hills, the gravity of the situation became clearer. Everything within was burnt beyond recognition; only the blackened walls still stood.

Ma told me to stay in the yard, but I had to see. They found what was left of the bodies: Mass John in the living room, Miss Daisy in the bedroom. Then I found her – Elizabeth. She was curled up and contorted. It was awful. A stream of tears flowed down my face as I looked at Elizabeth and as they got to my chin, they fell gently, tap, tap, tap on her corpse. Over in the corner, the rays of the morning sun beamed on a metal object which flickered. I went over and lifted the burnt board from off it and there was the mirror that she once used as she combed her dark, flowing, curly hair. The frame and handle were embellished with gold vines and flowers and a large E, written in cursive, was on the back. I picked it up and put it in the pocket of my dress.

'Essie!!' echoed Ma's voice which jolted me from my quiet contemplation. 'What mi tell you to do? You never hear to stay in di yard? Puppa Jezas, give mi strength to deal wid you! I going have to wash off this destruction off a you now! Come pickney!' With that said, she grabbed me by the hand and stormed out of the burnt out structure.

I could bathe myself, but that morning Ma made sure she did. She filled the old metal bath pan with all sorts of bush and oils. It smelled funny.

'Come, take off you clothes and go in.'

I complied, carefully putting down my dress so that the mirror wouldn't hit the floor. 'Mi child,' she said as she poured the warm water over me. 'You too young to understand all a dis, but I want no harm to come to you. You and di child was playmate. Same in life, same in death. They die a wicked death. Tings will never be di same, until they soul find rest. God, He knows what going to happen because a dis. Somebody going pay di price for it, you mark my word.'

She put a red nightie on me and burned some frankincense and myrrh in a small pot and opened the Bible to Psalm 91 and placed it beside my head on the bed. She used some olive oil and made the sign of the cross on my forehead and said, 'Sleep mi child. Di Lord watch over you.' But how could I sleep given what had happened the night before? My mind drifted back to the scene and a stream of tears cascaded down my face.

***

It was a mystery how the fire started. The adults spoke about it in hushed tones in the days that followed. Everyone drew their own conclusions about what happened. Miss Cindy came to look for Ma one day. In those times children were not entertained while adults talked, but I had my ways. Unknown to Ma, I inched up behind the front door while they talked on the verandah.

'What a ting eh Becka? Mass John, Miss Daisy and poor Elizabeth just gone like dat, burn to ash? I never know I would ah live to see some ting like dis!'

Island Voices

'Only God He knows Cindy. Only God He knows.'

'You know what they saying?'

'Who? And bout what?'

'People Becka! You always do like you lost to the world too much!'

'Eeeeh.'

'Yes, you do! Any ways, they fingering Manny for it.'

'Manny?'

'Yes! They say a him do it!'

'Cindy, you know you no fi talk after people! Listen to youself! Wah reason Manny would have fi kill Mass John? Him grow mongst wi from him likkle til now, nobaddy no know him as dat!'

'Becka! You and I know seh if you no mash ants you no see him gut! And if it no go so, it go near so. You know seh Mass John did have a piece a land round a William Thomas Hill right?'

'Right.'

'You memba when dem did a tief cow hard?'

'Eeeeh.'

'Well people seh that Mass John happen to catch Manny, Daphne and Jigga planning to move Georgie's cow over to dem side.'

'All I know, Cindy. I stay far from what don't concern me. You see weh mi live, far outta all harm's reach.'

'Same ting mi tell you, lost to di world! But as you know, people business is not my own. I just tell you since wi changing thoughts and di matter come up. Well Becks, mi have quite a few tings to do today, so I bes go down di hill. If I don't see you in the lamp, I see you in di wick.'

'Yes Cindy, walk good.'

'Aye sah, when is not one ting is di odda. Well if a so it go, God naw sleep and what done in di dark mus come to light,' Ma muttered to herself as she watched Miss Cindy leave.

***

Days passed. Buckston Hill was quiet and quaint by day but harrowing by night. Elizabeth's screams pierced through the night air and the crackling sound of the fire could be heard for miles around even though nothing was burning. Those who dared passed the house at night saw shadows moving throughout the house. They reported seeing Elizabeth in a white night gown just staring at them from the top floor. People claimed that they saw Mass John riding his mule as he would early in the morning. Everyone was tormented. Only the brave walked by the house after dark and before dawn. The children ran past when they went to the shop and Ma walked around the yard reciting a psalm or just talking to herself when she felt the need. Then the dreams started.

In my dreams Elizabeth would be in the burnt out rubble of her home calling me. 'Essie, I want to show you something. Come with me,' she said, as she stretched out her hand for me to take it, just as she used to when she was showing me around her house or when she got new clothes from England. I would jump from my sleep drenched in sweat, my heart pounding in my chest and covered in goosebumps. Whenever I had the dreams, I would pull the sheet over my head and hug Ma tightly, even though I know she didn't like it. 'Pickney, you want to cut off mi circulation?' she would ask, but what could I do? I was afraid. I didn't know what to do or what to say.

Ma couldn't deal with my tremors anymore and one morning at breakfast after a rather tumultuous night she asked, 'What troubling you child?' I was hesitant. I didn't want her to think that I was mad. 'Essie, di only way you can get help is if you open

Island Voices

you mout and talk. Speak di truth and speak it ever, cost it what it will,' she coaxed.

'Is Elizibet, Ma. Every night I dream-see har a call me, seh she want show me something.'

'Rock of ages clef for me!' Ma exclaimed with her hand on her head. 'Trouble is at mi door Lawd!'

'But I don't go wid har, Ma!' I reassured. 'I know she dead and I don't want she draw mi weh.'

'Same in life, same in death child.'

A few days later, Ma woke me up in the wee hours of the morning and under the cover of darkness we journeyed through the bush. It felt like we were walking for miles until we came upon a house. Under the flame of the bottle torch, Ma held my hand as we went around some white enamel basins filled with water nestled among several croton plants. Some of the basins had clear glass bottles in them, also full. We encircled it six times and on the seventh time a brown, diminutive woman came to the door. She had two huge plaits of white hair on either side of her head which protruded from her headtie and fell on her shoulders. 'Come in,' she said. She took us to an old table that had three chairs set around it to sit.

'The spirit follow unnu here you know. Di likkle girl seh she want to rest but not until she finish wid har business here on the earth.'

'So what dat mean, Madda? And what dat have to do wid Essie?'

'Give me you hand child,' she requested and I obliged. She held my hand and surveyed my palm. 'Di dead and di living not much different you know. You and di likkle girl was fren in life, same in death. She restless and she want to be free. You have something for her, hmmmm, a looking glass. You will need to use it.'

She got up from her seat and took a necklace made of John Crow beads from off a nearby shelf. 'So what I supposed to do now Madda? Is mi one gran pickney. Har madda dead from she three year old and is me and har and Massa God,' Ma said. 'Well, mi child, there is nothing that anyone can do but wait. Di spirit muss have its way. Don't be afraid child, she won't harm you. She just need help and you is the only one that can do that. Wear dis at all times and you will be alright,' she said as she placed the necklace around my neck. 'As soon as she do what she want, she will leave.'

***

I went straight to the old trunk, underneath the bed where I hid the mirror after the visit. My hands shook and my heart raced in anticipation. I raised it slowly but I couldn't see anything. There was no reflection. It was just cloudy. I put it back in the trunk. Days passed without a dream or a whisper from Elizabeth. 'Maybe Madda got it wrong,' I thought. 'Maybe, the necklace kept her away too.' Then one night, I took out the mirror just to look at it and admire its beauty. When I raised it to my face, the mist was dispelled. I could see my reflection and Elizabeth standing behind me. I dropped the mirror. To my surprise it did not break. I looked behind me but saw no one. Immediately, a chill ran down my spine, my head felt like it tripled in size and I was awash with goosebumps. I took up the mirror and looked again. There she was, just like people said, in a white nightie.

'You can only see me through the glass, Essie,' she said smiling in my dream.

'W-w-what you want Elizibet?' I stuttered. Her countenance changed.

'I want you to help me get revenge. I should not have died. My parents should not have died. They took my life from me and I want them to feel my wrath, Essie! Their life for mine!'

'Who you talking bout, Elizibet?'

'You will find out soon enough, everybody will. Tomorrow, I want you to go to my house and take three stones and place them on the highest window ledge you can find. Break a branch of the croton in the front yard and hang it in the window. Come Essie, there is something you must see.'

She extended her hand. The next thing I know, I was in her house just like it was before the fire, perched up behind a door in the living room. I saw Manny, Deacon Brown and Jigga in a heated conversation.

'Naw sah, mi no inna dat!' Jigga quipped.

'As far as I am concerned, nothing happened. I am giving you gentlemen a fair deal – report to the station or I will,' Mass John said calmly.

'Me no know bout you but in my case prison did mek fi dawg. I preffa dead fuss before mi set foot in dat place. Mass John, you tink you a smaddy true you have it eeh? You tink you sorry fa days work cudda mek me have money inna my pocket? I shudda poll you and di cow wah night!' Manny retorted.

'Fellas, fellas!! Calm down man! John, ther mus be a betta way dan dis. Imagine how it ago look fi see di upstanding young man dem and me, a deacon behind di bars! And Rosie a cook Sunday dinner carry come give a big man like me! Di disgrace John! Tink about di disgrace! See and blind, hear and deaf John!' Deacon Brown beseeched.

'Listen to yourself Brown! You can't be serious!' Mass John bellowed as he rose to his feet. He looked Deacon Brown dead in the eyes. 'See and blind? What of the farmers who have lost heads of cattle and goats to you and your cronies? And then you walk to church with your Bible in your hand on a Sunday! You should be ashamed of yourself! You're a blood thirsty snake that bruises the heel! Let him that is filthy, be filthy still!'

'Well den. I guess our business here is done,' Jigga remarked as he got up from the table. Manny got up next and turned to walk away but in the blink of an eye, he turned around and slashed Mass John's throat. Jigga inflicted the next wound straight through the chest. Mass John collapsed on the floor.

Deacon Brown was petrified. 'What unnu do dat for? Unnu mad? Puppa Jezas tek di case and gi mi di pilla!'

'Shet you mout Brown and come! Unless you want go wid him,' Manny declared. The three men hurried outside and closed the door. Manny and Jigga came back shortly after and started dousing the house with kerosene, starting from the living room and going all the way up the stairs. When they came back down to the living room, they lit a bottle torch, dropped it on the carpet, locked the door and left. There was a mighty whoosh as fire met accelerant and within minutes we were surrounded by flames. I saw Elizabeth running through the house looking for a way of escape. The searing heat and the marauding flames leapt high as they ran along the path that was made for them, sealing all exits, blocking her every move. Her last ditch attempt was a bedroom window on the top floor but the window was jammed and only one window pane barely moved. She let out the most gut-wrenching scream which pierced the air. I covered my ears and closed my eyes tightly. She took me by the shoulders and whispered, 'Open your eyes Essie. It is time. You must tell them to meet me here at dusk.'

My eyes popped open and a deep gasp for breath signalled my return. It was daybreak. 'Essie! Essie!' Ma said running over to the bedside. 'Tank you Jezas, thank you Lawd!' said Miss Cindy. 'Come Cindy, help mi lif her and put the pilla at har head. Carry some water fi she drink.' I was listless and unable to speak for quite a while. Worry was etched on their faces. When my strength and voice came back, I told them what happened.

'Well child, you have work to do,' Ma said. She and Miss Cindy followed me to the house and I did as Elizabeth had said. Then one by one we went to the house of each man. Needless to say, everybody ran us from their yard. Deacon Brown rebuked us in Jesus' name. According to him I was a 'false prophet' and a 'rabble-rouser that God would judge wickedly'.

It was all too much for my heavy heart which had dropped into my stomach at this point. I fell to the ground in the middle of the dirt track which led to Deacon's yard and I cried a bitter cry. When I stopped, Miss Cindy pulled her handkerchief from her bosom and wiped my face. Ma bent down in front of me and said, 'Esmeralda Johnson, you have nothing to cry fa! You talk di truth and dat is di most important ting. Never be ashamed child of what you did. Never be afraid to talk di truth, cost it what it will. Some will love you, some will hate you but you get a job to do and you do it. Whatever happen after dis is dem fault. You mek mi head hold up today Essie! I prouder today fi call you mi granddaughta. You madda wudda proud too. When men on earth have done their best, angels in heaven can do no more.' Her words rolled the dark clouds away and put a smile on my face. 'Dat is my Essie! Come you getting two extra dumplin in you plate tonight.'

'Yes Ma!'

Ma cooked early that night; she would not be caught dead outside after dusk. She was not taking any chances either. She mixed some red oak and painted it on the lintels and the door posts. I don't think anyone slept a wink that night. The dogs howled and barked all night as some ferocious winds swept Buckston Hill. As dusk turned to dawn, tranquillity gave way to discord. You could hear the wailing from miles around. 'Hear deh sah!' Ma exclaimed. Not too long after Miss Cindy raced into the yard, breathless.

'Becka!! Becka ohh!! Jezas Gad Almighty!! Judgement in Buckston Hill!'

'Cindy, wah kind a noise you a mek inna mi yaad so early inna di mawnin?'

'Death and destruction Becka!! All a dem dead till dem teet kin. Is a sight to behold Becka!! Di tree man dem suck out dry, dry as chip. You affi come look!'

'I don't have to go anywhere, Cindy. I staying right here. Every dog have him day and every man have him six o'clock. I have nothing else to say on the matter.'

'Arite Beck. I hear you. I goin back out di road. I will let you know how it go.' And with that said, she took off like a bolt of lightning.

'Essie!'

'Yes Ma!'

'Put on you clothes, take di looking glass and come. We have one thing left to do.'

Ma and I went through the short cut to the Anderson's house. 'Go put it back right where you find it and come.'

As I exited the house, I looked back and there was Elizabeth in the window of the top floor smiling. 'Come Essie,' Ma beckoned. I looked at Ma and when I looked back Elizabeth was gone.

***

'Who is buried here, Grandma?'

'She was about your age, thirty-five years ago today. The calamity of her death was unforgettable.'

MY PINK COCOYEA BROOM

Sherena Christmas

I SLAMMED MY bedroom door, and roughly turned the knob to the locked position. Ordinarily, at this point, Daddy would have immediately taken the door off the hinges for at least a week. Today was different; both my parents stood outside the locked door and tried to coax me to unlock it ... their attempts, futile.

'Majorie, come let's talk nuh,' Mammy urged me.

I remained silent.

Many girls may be excited to buy their first bra, but I had no interest in this activity. My mom insisted that it was 'absolutely necessary at this point', but twelve-year-old me was adamant that I was 'not going to buy no stupid bra!'.

***

My thoughts drifted back to the third Saturday in October last year; every detail was permanently etched on my memory. That afternoon, I remember the house phone rang. My grandmother on my mother's side – Mama, I called her – answered the call.

'Yes. Uh huh. Okay. Monday morning, God's will, eight o'clock. Thank you doctah. Ba bye.'

Mama hung up the phone and sighed hard. After a few pensive minutes, though, she was out of that mood, and cheery once again.

'Majo,' she called me. 'Let's go and make the cocoyea brooms nuh doo-doo.'

I loved when Mama called me 'Majo' and 'doo-doo'.

'Yes, Mama,' I said.

Making cocoyea brooms was a significant part of Mama's and my life. When I had school, I could only assist Mama on Saturdays, but during the summer, I could help her during the weekdays too. Then, on the fourth Saturday of every month, Mama and I would go to the Roseau Market to deliver cocoyea brooms to customers who had placed orders. We always made some extra brooms, and we always sold all the brooms, and left the market with orders for the following month.

'This is how I makin' my money, and, as my own grandmoda taught me, I teach my Majo,' Mama always said.

Indeed, the time we spent making cocoyea brooms strengthened my bond with Mama. I made some money from this activity too, and Mama would take me to the Credit Union once a month to save my earnings.

That Saturday, we aimed to make a total of forty cocoyea brooms. I held Mama's hand as we walked down the gently-sloping, cobblestone path that led from our house to our backyard, adjacent to the sea. Our cocoyea broom factory was a wooden stall which housed a long bench made of bamboo and plywood, and the entire structure was covered by an overlapping roof made of interwoven palm leaves. My father had proudly crafted this structure in the backyard, facing the sea, so that Mama would have a comfortable outdoor space with a scenic view where she could engage in her favourite occupation.

That day, the sun was shining brightly, but the moderate sea breeze was strong enough to offset much of the effects of the high temperatures. The bayfront was lively; villagers were enjoying sea-bathing, fishing and building sandcastles amidst lively conversation and boisterous laughter.

Our neighbour, Joachim, had cut off the coconut fronds for us a few days before, so they were already on the ground in our cocoyea broom factory.

'The brooms make best when the leaflets still ah likkle green, but dry enough.' This was Mama's secret to ensuring the durability and longevity of her products.

We sat on the bench and began making the cocoyea brooms. First, using a very sharp cutlass, Mama adeptly cut off the leaflets from the main stalks of the fronds. Next came my favourite part – stripping the coconut leaflets to retrieve the cocoyea sticks. Once I was old enough, Mama had carefully explained and demonstrated this part to me.

'Hold the knife away from your body, doo-doo, and strip off de boff sides of de leaflet to get de hard centa stick,' she had said.

I was now an expert at this.

As we stripped the leaflets, we placed the cocoyea sticks in a neat pile, using Daddy's new wheelbarrow as a container. We worked well together, Mama and I, and we enjoyed lively conversation while we worked.

'Soon you will be in high school, Majo,' Mama said proudly. 'I can't wait to take picture with you on your first day. I know it will be de first day of many great things to come.'

'Yes, Mama,' I replied with a smile.

Mama was proud of me. She encouraged and supported me, and she expected the best of me. Most of all, Mama was a good example to me; she was hardworking, humble, honest and oh so brave and strong.

About an hour had passed and we had made significant progress; we had just a small pile of leaflets left to shred.

'Go and get a bottle of water and a glass for Mama please, doo-doo,' Mama said to me.

I went upstairs to fetch it, room temperature water; Mama never drank water from the fridge. I brought her the bottle of water and poured her two glasses that she gulped down one after the other. I took a few sips too, and we carried on with our work.

Mama was diagnosed with breast cancer when I was six years old. At that time, I was still too young to strip the coconut leaflets, and definitely too young to understand Mama's illness. However, I remember that she had to go into the hospital for a few months, and that disrupted our time making cocoyea brooms. Then she had surgery and came home with one breast. Mama didn't know this, but about two years after her surgery, she had left her door slightly ajar while getting dressed one day, and I had peeped through and saw her condition; her left breast looked normal, but where her right breast should have been, I saw a big scar. I remember covering my mouth so that Mama would not hear my gasp. I was only about eight years old at the time, but that visual made it clearer to me that Mama had suffered greatly with this disease. The feeling then, was bittersweet; I had felt sad and helpless, but also grateful to still have my Mama with me. For a while, she was bald-headed. Mama didn't have insurance, so we got donations, and used her savings from her cocoyea broom sales to meet the exorbitant cost of her medical treatment.

'Mama, what did the doctor say?' I asked, referring to the phone call she had received just before we came downstairs.

'Nothing, doo-doo, bagay bon, Bondyé bon ... things good, God is good,' she told me in our local Creole parlance.

I had mostly been afraid to ask Mama about her illness. That day, I wasn't.

'Mama, how you get breast cancer?' I asked.

Mama smiled at me.

'Well, doo-doo, the doctahs say there can be different causes. It could be something in your genes, or your lifestyle. And then, de cells in the breast start to grow big big big, and they make a lump, and that destroys your health,' Mama explained.

Island Voices

'Oh my,' I said. I soaked in every word. 'So, is that why the doctors removed one of your breasts, to remove the cancer?' I asked.

'Yes, doo-doo,' said Mama. 'De surgery is called a mastectomy.'

'Mas-tec-to-my,' I repeated the word very slowly.

'Yes, doo-doo. Then I had to do chemo ... chemotherapy, jus' to make sure all de cancer was gone. So that medicine is what made me lose my hair,' Mama explained as she ran her fingers through her now bouncy, natural, grey curls.

'Oooooooohhhhhhhhh! Mama, so how it feeling to have one breast?'

Mama chuckled. 'Well, they give me a special bra, so it make going out very comfortable. De hospital help me plenty too, because all of this can affect your mental health, and make you question your identity as a woman,' Mama said. 'But, every day, I look at my scar and I smile. It's a sign of my survival. And, of course, I am happy that I survived to see my Majo grow into a big, beautiful girl.' Mama's face lit up with a big grin.

I smiled warmly at this information shared by Mama effortlessly and freely, and I felt very grateful for this.

At about 4.00 p.m. we finally finished stripping all the coconut leaflets. Mama and I gathered the cocoyea strips into bundles of a predetermined size. Then, Mama tied each bundle with a piece of black rope, and she trimmed the edges so that the brooms were even. We achieved our goal of making forty cocoyea brooms that day, and there was still a small bundle of cocoyea sticks left.

'Cocoyea broom not just for sweeping you know doo-doo,' Mama said. 'You can use them for protection from bad spirits. And, of course, my favourite thing to do is make cocoyea brooms with you, so it's a sign of our bond. Let's make one for you to keep in your room.'

I smiled and nodded in agreement.

Mama gathered the remaining cocoyea sticks into a bundle, tied them together, and used the cutlass to level them as she had done before. Just then, my father came downstairs.

'Mikey, take de pail of pink paint in de storeroom for me please son-son.'

Daddy nodded, and fetched the pail and placed it in front of Mama.

'Mesi,' she said, expressing her thanks to him.

'Pink is de colour for breast cancer awareness, and this month, October, is Breast Cancer Awareness Month,' Mama told me.

She opened the pail of paint and placed the broom to stand in it. The entire cocoyea broom was submerged in the five gallons of pink paint.

'A pink cocoyea broom, de first of it kind,' Mama said smiling.

We packed our forty cocoyea brooms for sale into three large cardboard boxes, which we covered and placed in our storeroom downstairs. The following Saturday, Daddy would have to take Mama and me to the Roseau Market to sell our products. Proud of our afternoon's work, Mama and I sat and chatted a bit more for a few minutes. The collage of colours in the sky announced the sunset, which indicated to us that it was time to wrap up our outdoor activities for the day.

Mama put on a glove on her right hand, and then removed the cocoyea broom from the pail of pink paint. She smiled, evidently happy with her novel creation. Then, Mama looked around our yard.

'Uhm, okay... let's place this concrete block on de ole piece of plywood, then put de broom to stand in de hole of de block so that it can dry,' Mama said.

I organised the structure in our cocoyea broom factory, and Mama placed the broom in one hole of the block.

'This is your pink cocoyea broom, Majo. May it always remind you of my love for you, doo-doo,' Mama said as she hugged me close. Then, she held my hand, and we went upstairs for dinner and bedtime.

Four days later, I was awakened from my sleep by a commotion in the house. I checked the time on my desk clock –1.25 a.m. The ambulance had come to get Mama; apparently, she had fainted while going to the bathroom. My mom went with Mama in the ambulance. Daddy took me to his mom, Grandma Edna, and then he went to meet my mom at the hospital. Grandma Edna put me to bed, but I didn't sleep. I had an eerie feeling.

My parents came to collect me at about 9.00 a.m. that morning. They told me that Mama was admitted to the hospital and had to stay there for some urgent treatment.

My parents went to visit Mama every day at the hospital.

'When Mama gets a little stronger, we will take you to see her,' Mammy had promised me.

So every day I would give my parents small notes and cards to read to Mama at the hospital. I remained hopeful that Mama would get better and that I would see her again soon.

One evening, about two weeks after Mama was admitted to the hospital, the house phone rang. Mammy answered the phone, and as she spoke, she seemed frantic, although she tried to hide it. Once again, my parents rushed me to Grandma Edna's house, and told me they had to go to the hospital to check on

Mama. They came to get me the next morning, and to deliver the somber news that Mama had passed away.

In the days between Mama's death and her funeral, family and friends had gathered at our home, for prayer, conversation and to assist our family with funeral preparations. The adults spent many hours together at our dining table, talking through the pain that breast cancer had brought to our family over the years. My grandaunt Maria, Mama's sister, had passed away after a battle with breast cancer about two years before Mama's diagnosis. My older cousin, Jacob, a well-known banana farmer in our community, had also been in remission for a few years after battling breast cancer.

I overheard my mother talking one evening, and I tiptoed closer to the dining room, and hid just outside the doorway to listen. Mammy recalled that it was Dr John, Mama's oncologist, who had called Mama the afternoon we made my pink cocoyea broom. The hospital had been trying to convince Mama to come in to discuss an experimental drug, but Mama had refused to keep her appointments. The cancer had returned, and had spread to her left breast, but Mama was adamant that she was not going to do more treatments.

'Twòp lajan, twòp douleh – too much money, too much pain,' my mother recalled Mama saying in our local Creole language.

'Did Mama know she was going to die?' I repeated this question to myself as I eavesdropped on a conversation that I clearly was not supposed to hear.

Mammogram ... that word came up a lot as the adults spoke. My mom and her sisters always went to get their mammograms together.

'All our results are good so far,' my mother said to the group of adults seated around the table that evening.

Island Voices

'We can't predict the future, but surely, early detection can save lives,' my aunty Martha said.

One week after Mama's death, I went downstairs to fetch my pink cocoyea broom. It was dry, and very pink. I brought it upstairs and placed it next to my dressing table. It had stayed in the same spot ever since.

***

I sighed as I brought my thoughts back to the present. Tears dashed down my blushed cheeks as I sat on my bed and stared at my pink cocoyea broom.

Through Mama's experience, I now had a lot more knowledge about breast cancer. I also had many more questions.

What about my mother, was this cancer 'in her genes' as well? Would I eventually lose my mother to breast cancer? Would I also have to watch her suffer, the way I watched Mama suffer? Was breast cancer 'in my genes' too? I pondered on all these questions very often.

On my twelfth birthday, my parents had granted me a bit of unsupervised access to the internet. *How to not get breasts?* – I had Googled this several times. My hypothesis was that if I didn't have breasts, I couldn't get breast cancer. The internet didn't give me a workable solution quick enough, and mother nature was right on cue to usher me into puberty. To me, this bodily change was weakening my already diminished defence against my biggest enemy. So, for the past two weeks, whenever my mother brought up the topic of shopping for bras, I would have an emotional outburst.

Mama had always been the antidote to my tantrums.

'What would Mama say to me today?' I whispered to myself.

Several minutes had passed, and I was still staring at my pink cocoyea broom. Now, I could feel Mama's presence near me, comforting me, strengthening me. I think Mama appeared to me ... although I'm not sure. I think I saw her face, and I think I heard her voice. Whatever it was, I felt Mama with me.

'What would Mama say to me today?' I whispered to myself again.

Mama always celebrated my growth. No occasion was too small for a party, and she relished new experiences. Mama never worried about the future; she lived in the present. I couldn't bring Mama back, but I could honour her by the way I chose to live my life.

'I will not be afraid,' I repeated over and over, softly.

I grabbed a napkin from my dressing table and wiped my face, and I spent a few more minutes with my thoughts, and just staring at my pink cocoyea broom.

'This is your pink cocoyea broom, Majo. May it always remind you of my love for you, doo-doo.' I remembered Mama's words to me.

I sighed, stood up, opened the door of my bedroom, and walked into the dining room. My parents were sitting at the table, conversing softly and holding hands. I looked at them and nodded. They understood.

'I'm sorry for slamming the door,' I apologised to my parents sincerely.

'Thank you, sweetie,' Daddy acknowledged me.

'Let's get a pink bra, Mammy,' I said.

My mother held my hand securely and guided me out the front door, as if she was concerned that I might change my mind.

'Hmmm, let's discuss it in the car,' she said with a smile.

Island Voices

ESCAPE

Rosetta Thomas

'HELLO, PA, THE aeroplane is about to take off now, so I will see you shortly,' I said in my polished British accent as I fastened my seat belt, ahead of my ten-hour flight.

'Alright mi granddaughter. I will leave out in a few hours to catch the country bus to Kingston,' he responded in a very frail voice.

'Ok. See you soon and love you,' I responded.

'And by the way,' he quickly added, as I was about to disconnect the call, 'mi wearing a grey Rasta wig; mi beard is now grown and I dyed it in grey with streaks of black ...'

'No problem at all, Pa,' I replied. 'I've got to go now though ... so see you later,' I finished before terminating the call and turning off all my electronic devices.

This was my second trip to Jamaica, and my only mission was to go for my grandfather, Pa, so that he could join us in living in England. Pa is the only connection we have on the island and so his impending migration will close this chapter of our lives ... forever. As the plane was about to take off, I started to wonder to myself if at his age, he would be able to manage the brutal British weather. He was not only old but frail, as he suffered a lot of hardship since Ma, his wife who was also my grandmother, passed away years ago. Notwithstanding the weather, England was bound to be a game changer for him, as he would have an opportunity to enjoy his last days with his family before he died.

My name is Grace English and I was born in England to a 15-year-old teenage immigrant, who had earlier conceived me in the beautiful island of Jamaica. After my mother's pregnancy came to light, my grandparents sent her to live with her aunt in England, where she resided as an undocumented citizen for several years before being regularised by the courts. Before leaving Jamaica, my mom served as prefect at her high school, contestant for her school's quiz team, and she was also a prolific debater who participated in national and regional debating competitions.

She was a young lady with great potentials and great ambitions; however, her dreams and aspirations were snatched out of her hands when an unwanted pregnancy forced her to become a teenage mother. In spite of all this, she still managed to single-handedly raise me, gave me the education I needed to become a computer engineer, and also get a college degree of her own.

I know very little about the sperm donor who contributed the seed for my conception. From what I heard, he was a notorious don man who made demands on all the young girls living in the community of Hopeville from the moment their breasts started to bud. Regardless of whether or not they consented, they had to give him full access to their bodies, and their parents had to keep quiet and defend him publicly if needs be. I crossed paths with him only once and this was on my first trip to Jamaica, when my mother and I travelled to attend Ma's funeral.

As I unbuckled my seatbelt in the aeroplane so I could comfortably extend my long legs, my mind reflected on the very unusual meeting with my father, and the life-changing events which followed. I vividly recall this taking place on the gloomy moon-lit night of Ma's wake, which had preceded the day slated for her funeral. Precisely, it was just before dawn when the thick misty blanket of sadness which hung in the atmosphere stood still in the home. The yard was busy with people walking to and fro, but around that time, I was lost in thought as I looked through my late grandmother's bedroom window, watching the way the shadows of the visitors moved up and down. My attention was, however, drawn to a man appearing out of nowhere, walking briskly towards the house.

Almost immediately, he captured the attention of all the persons in the yard. The women who were busy sharing and distributing food and drinks suddenly resigned from their duties, staring at him as he walked towards the main entrance. The young men playing dominoes paused and stared at him. As he walked pass them, they said in a chorus, 'Hail, God Father the lion,' while giving him a brief hand salute. In addition to this, the children who were hugging themselves to escape the coldness of the night as they sat on the rocks, stood up as he approached them, and the elderly men who were chanting psalms, became silent, taking off their hats to acknowledge his presence.

Wiping the soggy tears from her swollen eyes for the billionth time, my mother who was leaning on my shoulders suddenly gasped and whispered, 'This is trouble.'

Without looking at her, I questioned, 'What do you mean, Mom?'

Giving a big sigh, she responded, 'We are in big trouble,' before disappearing out of the room.

I turned around to see Pa, who had been outside with the elderly men, hurrying inside with sorrow in his leaf-shaped eyes, while my mother, who had met him on the veranda, walked soundlessly behind him. I could see the thick lines on his forehead rising and his high cheek bones seemed to become more apparent.

'What's going on?' I asked.

'Hide yourself—,' he said to me while quickly slipping inside the closet.

But before I could move, I was staring into the face of the stranger, as he stood blocking the doorway. Opening her mouth in fright, my mother held on to my waist with her trembling hands as I stood confused.

For a while the stranger seemed to inhale the pungent scent of rum and smoke coming from the centre of the wake, mixed with the scent of perfume from my late grandmother's bedroom. He then started to study me for a moment or two, before taking off the broad-brimmed felt hat that had swallowed his head. I could clearly see the wrinkles on his freckled face, which announced death and destruction, as he pushed aside his jacket to expose and bring our attention, to a small hatchet that was firmly held in place by his waistband.

'Long run, short catch!' he said with a big grin on his face, while slowly clapping his hands and looking at my mother. 'You ran away from me the Don Gorgon for so many years ... but not to worry cos absence truly makes my heart grow fonder,' he mocked.

While looking at me from head to toe, he exclaimed, '... Bless my eyesight! I live to see mi long lost daughter! What a way she looks just like me!'

Turning to my mom, he continued. 'You hid her from me all these years. You did not even call and let me, the Don Gorgon, know whether you had a boy or girl. Mi care about the fruits of my loins you know. Mi is a lion but mi is a very tender lion.'

The room was as still as death as mom and I stood awestruck, trembling in fright. With a deadly smile, he continued further, '... You know, old fire stick is veeery easy to catch! As of tonight, you will be my new queen! And I can get to spend time and know mi daughter. Both of you coming home with me and you not going back to England ...'

Island Voices

Bursting into a storm of weeping, my mother held onto me and screamed out, '... Please ... have mercy God Father ... Please ... have mercy. We have built our lives in England. We have to go back home,' she finished, sobbing.

'Hush up!' he stopped her.

'Mi is the original and only Don Gorgon in Hopeville so whatever mi say is final,' he finished at the top of his voice, while beating his chest with his right hand to demonstrate the power he commanded.

He stepped forward, pulled out the hatchet and raised it threateningly in the air towards my mother.

'Hand over all your papers,' he demanded. 'You think you can disrespect the Don Gorgon and get away? Give me your passports and aaaaaall your money!' he shouted.

By this time, I could smell the queer scent of confusion permeating the atmosphere, as my mother buried herself at his feet weeping. I opened my mouth to scream, but instead I heard a loud explosion from a single shot, so loud that it surprised the stranger for a second or two as he stood motionless, before falling face down, to the ground. Looking across the room, I saw Pa, kneeling down with an old rusty gun in his hands, which was still emitting fumes.

'That is for taking advantage of my daughter ... you Don Gorgon,' my grandfather said mockingly, while looking at his lifeless body.

For a moment or two, it felt like a dream. However, the reality was that God Father, the roaring lion of Hopeville, who had terrorised my family for years, was slain. This is the man who impregnated my mother against her will; whose demands forced her to run off to a foreign land; and who, a few moments earlier, was demanding our travel documents and money, so he could interrupt our plans to return home to England. This is the man who was my father. As I stared at his lifeless body, I could smell the sweet fragrance of the blooming flowers which rose through the stillness of the dawn, to announce the freshness of an emerging day.

A few moments later, the dead silence was interrupted.

'People! Peooooooople! Come quick!,' cried a one-footed-man who had peeped inside the house. 'God Father get shot! Dem shot up the Don,' he announced to the community while swinging himself on his crutches.

Before long, all the mourners at the wake converged on the scene. Tears of agony went up to heaven as all the people who earlier were mourning for Ma, started mourning for the Don. They quickly took up his lifeless body and rushed to a car to take him to Kingston Public Hospital, to see if they could save any of the life that had just evaporated from his body.

Almost immediately, some young men and children started to throw glass bottles at us. We had to run for cover in one of the rooms and bolted the door behind us. Some of the men tried to kick in the door where we were hiding, and so we had to quickly pull furniture behind it for support.

'How comes unnu violate God Father?' asked a man in a very angry voice amidst the wailing of women. 'It is because of God Father why we can eat food and send we children to school,' he continued. 'What we going to do now?' he bemoaned, before releasing a long stream of expletives in the air.

'We going to burn unnu up tonight,' shouted another man in a distant voice.

Almost immediately, we heard a loud sound from the kitchen as the gas cylinder which was ignited by bottle bombs exploded, causing the house to be set on fire.

My heart pounded and I could see my entire life flashing before me in a split second. As I stared death in the face, I started to say my last prayers with all the strength I could muster. A few minutes later, we could hear sirens in the near distance, as police officers on patrol, who were alerted by the explosions, drove towards the house.

'Babylon ah come ...' shouted the people, running away as the police vehicle approached.

The police rescued us before the ravaging fire reached the room in which we took cover. We only sustained minor scorches from the heat of the flames as we tried to save some of our clothes and the metal safe in which the family traditionally kept all important documents.

Soon thereafter, a Fire Brigade unit pulled up to put out the fire, but they were of little help as they did not have enough water to put out all the blaze. Consequently, we had to watch as the family home and all its precious memories went up in flames and crumbled to the ground, room by room. The fire was finally extinguished by another fire truck which came on the scene to do cool-down operations. We were escorted out of the community by the police force with what was left of the belongings we were able to save and Pa was taken to the police station for questioning.

That night was the last time my family saw Hopeville, as we were banished from the community ... forever. Ma's funeral had to be postponed. Ultimately, we were not able to give her a respectable send-off, as she was buried four months later by the funeral parlour without a soul in attendance.

Pa eventually got off all charges on the grounds of self-defence. However, he had to run away to a remote district in Clarendon where he was marooned for the most part, sustained by a family friend. My mother and I came back to England and resumed life, but things were not the same as before, as we suffered a lot from the trauma we endured.

As I massaged my feet that were already numb from the long flight to Jamaica, my mind wandered as the pain I endured during those trying days flooded my heart. I closed my eyes tightly to fight the bitter tears forcing their way down my cheeks as reality began to set in. God Father had brought nothing but pain and sorrow in our lives, and although he is no longer alive, his many cronies on the island are bent on revenging his death. The reality was that I was en route to Jamaica for Pa, and I must ensure that we did not cross their path.

I was jolted back to reality by the voice of the air stewardess who was serving food.

'Are you okay, Madam?' she asked me, while giving me a napkin.

'I'm fine, thanks,' I replied, while wiping my teary eyes.

'What do you want to eat?' she continued.

'I'm fine with tea,' I replied with a broad smile.

My appetite had disappeared in thin air to the extent that I found the scent of the food being served, repulsive.

How can I eat when I am on this dangerous and uncertain expedition to bring Pa to England? I pondered in my mind.

Not long after that, I fell asleep. Some hours later, I was awakened by the voice of the pilot announcing that we were approaching the island of Jamaica. I looked through the window and from a distance, I saw my lush green island laying down in the midst of the ocean.

'Jamaica, you are such a beautiful country,' I said out loud. 'It is such a pity that I am robbed of your daily sunshine and have to live in the bitter cold of England,' I bemoaned.

Shortly after, the aeroplane touched down on Jamaican soil and then my heart began to beat faster and faster. 'This is it,' I said to myself. 'I must do this. I must get Pa … and we must get out alive.'

I passed through customs and exited the airport, chartered a taxi, and set out to the Kingston Secrets Hotel where I would be spending one night. There, I could finalise everything in a timely manner, and get Pa a comfortable bed to rest before our long flight to England. I reached the hotel in no time, and sure enough, Pa was there, sitting on a bench outside with his head buried on his knees, a brown crocus bag filled with white rum, honey and spices firmly placed on the seat beside him.

I exited the vehicle and hugged him so tightly that I could feel the rib-bones of his thin and frail body. I cried so much as I held him to my chest.

'Let's go,' Pa said, while picking up his bags.

'We have to make sure we are not spotted because the cronies of the late God Father have eyes aaaaaall over the country,' he finished in almost a whisper, while stretching out his arms to demonstrate his point.

'Yes, Pa,' I said, while holding on to his arms and helping him with his bags.

We went into the hotel lobby and joined the queue to book the room, but the line was moving slower than expected.

As I paced the floor and tried to catch up on the local news on my mobile phone, I felt the piercing eyes of someone watching me, with every move I made.

I looked up and made eye contact with a female security guard employed to the hotel. I vividly remembered her as the one who cooked the curried goat and white rice at Ma's wake years ago. She scanned us from head to toe with her fiery eyes, which were as still as death.

My heart skipped a beat. *Could it be that we are spotted?* I wondered, as I continued to look down at my phone while trying to avoid her stare.

In front of me were nine guests, but it felt like there were ninety-nine. I glanced out of the corner of my eyes just in time to see the security guard snapping a picture of us, before texting on her phone. Almost immediately, I could hear the sound of galloping horses in my chest as my heart rate increased in rapid proportion.

In less than 15 minutes, I noticed the presence of two men wearing dark glasses and dressed in black casual attire, walking around pacing the floor. Time was running out, but the universe stood still.

'I think we have been spotted!' I whispered to Pa.

'Kiss mi neck!' he exclaimed under his breath. 'That means we have to go now. Mi granddaughter, these people are daaaaangerous you know!' he said in a trembling voice with sorrow in his leaf-shaped eyes.

'I will take care of this, so don't worry. Just stay calm,' I reassured him, while trying to muster courage to disguise my fears.

It was finally my turn to book our room and so we approached the receptionist desk to have our transaction processed. When we were almost through, I quietly asked the receptionist in almost a whisper, 'Can I get a cab to go to the craft market please?'

'That is no problem at all,' she responded.

'In the meantime, I would like a porter to take both pieces of our luggage to our room,' I finished, while putting Pa's passport in my handbag.

'Okay, Madam. Your room is number 400. As requested, your belongings will be taken there. Cab number 5 is already on the outside. Do enjoy your stay with us and thanks for making it Kingston Secrets Hotel,' she stated, while giving us a smile.

As we finished the transaction and moved away from the receptionist station, I thought of how I could detract the men watching us, so they could not figure out my real intentions. I then spoke to Pa in an elevated, yet normal tone, so they could hear.

'I'm so hungry. Let's go to the restaurant and grab a bite.'

In no time, one of the strange men moved towards the restaurant door ahead of us, while his accomplice remained in the lobby, pacing the floor and pretending to scan through some tourist attractions on display. I stopped to pass time, pretending to search my handbag for something. When I realised that the accomplice in the lobby was distracted, I quickly tugged on Pa's hand and headed for the waiting cab.

'Driver ...' I said, trying to catch my breath. 'We are heading to Norman Manley International Airport.'

Looking down at my watch, I said to him, lying, 'We are running late for our flight.'

'I will pay you four times the amount if you get us there in 15 minutes,' I finished.

As the cab was driving out, I could see the two strange men running towards a black car.

The taxi cab in which we were travelling flew like an airplane on land, but by the time we had covered half of the journey, I could see that the black car trailing us was just two vehicles away. Not long after that, our driver disregarded the stop light, and their car, which by now had overtaken the two vehicles travelling before them, followed suit, and almost caused an accident, which slowed them down a bit.

'I think we are being followed by gun men!' I said frantically to the driver.

'Kiss mi neck!' exclaimed the driver. 'You know that my wife dreamt last night that gun men blow out mi car tyre?'

he continued while accelerating. 'But she prayed for me this morning so I'm not worried! ... Her prayer always works!' he boasted, while driving through the umpteenth stop light.

I suddenly heard a loud explosion. The men fired at our tyres but missed and the shots caught the tyres of an armoured vehicle transporting money. Before long, we heard a barrage of gunshots as the security men in the truck surprised the men chasing us and blew out their car tyres.

While our vehicle sailed towards Norman Manley International, I could hear sirens in the distance as the high-profile drama ensued. When we reached the airport, we breathed a sigh of relief.

'You know, it is my wife prayer that saved me today. I tell You! Her prayer always works,' exclaimed the taxi driver, who was as shaken as we were.

After paying him for his service and bidding him goodbye, I held on to Pa and we both walked inside the airport to try to arrange an earlier flight.

Eight hours later, we boarded a Boeing 747 airplane, however all our luggage, including those bags which held the spices Pa took from Clarendon, were still at Kingston Secrets Hotel in room 400. We had escaped with only the clothes on our back, my handbag, Pa's dirty handkerchief and our passports. I did not even have the coat that I brought for Pa to shield him from the bitter cold of London once we landed.

As the great giant Boeing 747 lifted her wings and flew away from the small green bed of land sitting in the ocean, I could not hold back the tears. I looked through the window and watched the island growing smaller and smaller as the plane rose higher and higher in the sky. We had escaped and flown away like a bird, far away from the traps and snares of the cronies of the late God Father, the roaring lion. *I love my country, the beautiful sunshine and the people, but how can we live as prisoners in our own country?* I pondered.

As I continued to reason in my mind, I turned to Pa and said, 'It is so sad that the loyal disciples of God Father decided to live their lives preserving his evil legacy and preaching his gospel of destruction.'

Looking at me with sorrow in his eyes, he responded, 'He lives on in the lives of these people, mi granddaughter, he lives on ... Even in death, God Father, the roaring lion, is still roaring. His legacy lives on,' he finished.

For a moment or two we remained silent as we pondered all the events which had led us to this point.

Minutes later, the frail teary voice of Pa broke the silence. 'I have a dream,' Pa said, with tears flowing down his cheeks. 'That one day, the people of Hopeville will be so enlightened ... that they will no longer call good evil and evil good.'

'I have a dream ...,' he continued, 'that one day ... our communities will no longer sacrifice its citizens on the altar of loyalty to dons. ... And I have a dream that the day will come when young ladies in inner-city communities will live their lives uninterrupted and free from the sexual exploitation of wicked men, like God Father.'

Pa buried his head on my shoulders as we both released our emotions in tears of agony.

Hours later, we landed at London Gatwick Airport. As Pa stepped on British soil for the first time, he took off his wig and threw it in a garbage bin. A heavy load was lifted from his shoulders and he seemed twenty years younger.

As we entered the waiting hall of the airport, my mom, who was advised earlier of the change in travel arrangements, ran towards us and we all hugged so tightly that we could feel the raw heat of our body temperatures.

When we finally stepped out into the bitter cold, I could see Pa's body shivering in rejection of the brutal British weather. A new day had dawned indeed! I knew Pa would have some challenges adjusting to his new life, but at least he would no longer need to hide from the faithful disciples of the late God Father, the roaring lion of Hopeville, whose roar was as powerful in death as it was in life.

RENT MONEY

Sharnna Archat Edmondson

COURTNEY JUMPED UP and down on the bed as the worn springs from the mattress screamed in agony. His sturdy little legs posed in splits as he reefed himself in the air and then nailed the landing. He kept his large brown eyes fixed at the door, ready to evade his rival at the turn of the doorknob.

'Boy get down from the bed!' Brenda shouted. 'Continue jumping like a frog, ah going to give yuh one slap, yuh going to see blinky, if yuh stay on the bed another second.'

At that remark, Courtney jumped off the bed and climbed through the window to get outside. Brenda smiled to herself from the narrow hallway as the suspicious actions of a loud thump made her recognise his exact actions. She walked to her room as a feeling of torpor possessed her. The bed was dishevelled and the pillows laid on the floor. She walked over to the window, then slightly shifted the white laced curtains and watched her son. He was playing by himself and for a moment she was happy, content even, for a healthy son. She cupped her chin with her hands and went into deep thoughts. She sighed and then shook her head slowly. The defeat climaxed into a debacle.

Lord how am I going to make it through this month? We have a little food, but the money is not enough for the rent. Please Father, send help. Work is very hard to get, but ah going down to the bureau agency tomorrow. I just need five days' work and that will cover rent and some food for next week. Lord, please allow me to get di secretary job that I interviewed for at the Housing Trust. Brenda's thoughts were interrupted as Courtney leapt from the small guava tree and onto a patch of grass.

'Merciful God! Courtney, get inside now!'

It was Monday and Brenda got up early as usual. She used a wet wash rag to clean-up Courtney, who was still sleeping. 'Come on Boy, wake up! Yuh going to stay with Aunty Vera today.' As soon as she said those words Courtney's eyes popped opened. He loved staying with Aunty Vera, who had four children of her own – Mahalia was twelve, Shawn was eleven, Stephen was nine and Kennedy (affectionately called 'Pops' or 'Popsicle' because he loved popsicles) was the same age as Courtney, six years old. Brenda was dressed in a brown and beige professional suit with brown high-heeled shoes. It was one of her best suits which hugged the curves of her body. She seemed a sculpted sight, debonair in the manner in which she walked, with bright white teeth that ignited affection and envy. She was a beautiful, chocolate woman with thick lips and curly, black hair.

Vera stood at her gate waiting. As Brenda approached, she started smiling. Vera was very thin and tall, but her curves were in all the right places. She had long legs, long curly hair, pearly white teeth and a light complexion. She stretched out her arms for Courtney and he ran into them. She kissed him on his cheek and again on his forehead and again on his neck.

'I am gonna eat this little one. He looks so delicious; I bet he will taste good.' Vera laughed as she teased Courtney. She looked at Brenda, smiling from ear to ear, and took a step back, 'Larks mi Sista, yuh look like yuh going to a big office today man.'

'Big office mi foot! Is down the bureau I going to see if any day's work available. The months rolling by quickly girl and mi short a rent again.'

'Don't worry Brends, mi feel say something soon come up. I feel like di Housing Trust job going to come true fi yuh man. See

Island Voices

dey, yuh finally finish the CPS course and nowadays dem big office employ people wid the certificate. So nuh worry man. Yuh soon gone clear! Michael Manley did a good ting fi Jamaicans when him government formed the Housing Trust. Girl, now is not like one time when is only high colour people get certain job. Yuh remember how every time Mama look pon di house a country, she always say, '76 was a good year! Mi can own mi likkle tattoo.' She giggled in her high pitch voice. 'Manley change that, and now all a we have a chance to shine man. Sis you going to get your chance to shine. Try hurry up and get di work cause a long time mi wan stop pay rent and own something fi myself.'

'Heh heh. Yuh a talk real girl. Bwoy V, I really hope so because I tell you girl, I need to have a permanent job with my pay check sure every month. Heh heh, a from we small yuh a talk bout owning yuh velovin. It going to happen. Ah speaking it into being. Anyway, I have to run. Early bird catch di most worms. Lata V.'

'Alright Sis lata, but remember these kind of jobs is for a very short time, this is not you.'

Brenda shook her head in agreement and prayed in her heart for that time to hurry along. She waved at Courtney, but he was too busy playing with his cousins to notice her.

She arrived early at the bureau, but already there were many women waiting. When she stepped in everyone looked at her and when she took a number, the stares coagulated in awes. One woman in a floral headtie shook her head from side to side, another one whispered, 'Nuh only helper work dem offa a da bureau ya? But see ya!' The woman pouted her mouth toward Brenda and the women burst into an uncontrollable laughter, followed by hissing of the teeth and stares from head to toe to match.

Brenda took her number and sat staring into space, avoiding eye contact. She was quite aware of what they were thinking, but she was always of the opinion that it did not matter what the job, one must always look presentable. She waited patiently as the numbers were called for registration. The receptionist, with no expression and no emotion, stood up holding a sheet of paper and started to call out the list of jobs from which the women could choose. Before Brenda could decide to accept, the other women who were more familiar with the system beat her to it. She began to wonder if she was listening keenly enough. The stiffed faced receptionist rose again, 'I have a job here from Mrs Mortimer. This is a cleaning and washing job.'

No one responded. Brenda found it strange that the receptionist called the name of the person, because she did not call the names of the others. Today a name was called. The receptionist called again, Brenda jumped up, but she realised no one was in a rush to get it. She whispered, 'Thank you Lord, yuh shut di demon dem mouth, because you want me to get this one.' Brenda smiled as she took the sheet with the address.

The woman in the floral headtie touched her hand, 'My girl, yuh teking it?'

'Yes miss,' Brenda replied. In her mind she said, 'then yuh tink mi a go give yuh it eh.'

Brenda was so happy that she got a job she was almost skipping out of the bureau. She looked at the address. It was in Havendale, not far from where she lived. She looked at the job, it was a three-day job paying a full week's salary. This was just what Brenda was hoping to get. She thought the job sounded onerous, but it was better than nothing. 'I better hurry and get started.' Brenda arrived at the gigantic blue gate; she pressed the buzzer at the gate. A coarse, elderly woman was sitting on the stretched veranda, but she did not move. Brenda pressed the buzzer again. The woman emerged from the chair and walked slowly over to the locked veranda grill. She seemed tiny compared to the house. It was a two-storey, white house with huge, unusual glass windows, finished with blue trimmings. The intricate grillwork looked luxurious and very expensive.

'I'm not deaf! Can you read? The sign says press and wait.' The English accent was so thick you could cut it with a knife. The woman beckoned to the gardener to open the gate for Brenda to enter, while she unlocked her grill. 'That will be all for today, Paul. Please lock the tools in the storeroom and leave immediately. I will see you again at six in the morning.' Brenda walked the long stretch to the house and stepped onto the veranda, embellished with potted plants, which were all so green and lush.

'Good day Miss. My name is Brenda.'

The woman stood and looked scornfully at Brenda from head to toe, then sucked spit through her teeth. The woman's hair was pristine and her long red nails arched like claws as she rubbed her fingers against her thumbs, her light complexion turned pink as her upside down smile and large grey eyes observed Brenda with disdain. Slowly, she asked, 'Are you here for the job?'

'Yes Miss' Brenda answered timidly.

'My name is Mrs Mortimer, wife of the late Dr William Mortimer, Distinguished Chair of the Department of Periodontology at Howard and then later he came home to offer his service at the Little Hearts Hospital. Have you ever heard of him?'

'No Miss.'

'I did not think so,' Mrs Mortimer snapped. 'I am a retired matron from the Jamaica Hospital.' Her English was impeccable and intimidating. Her voice echoed in a high pitched soprano ready to break glass. 'Right O, enough introductions, let me show you what to do. Before I do that, can you wash and clean a house properly?'

'Yes Miss. I was—'

Mrs Mortimer's hand swiped up quickly indicating that she should halt. Brenda stopped in surprise and decided not to prolong the conversation. She needed the money.

'Ok Miss, here I have some towels. I want them to be washed with your hands, do these first. This is the washroom and the soap and softener is right here,' Mrs Mortimer pointed to a shelf.

Brenda looked at the towels: there were two dozen coloured ones and another two dozen whites. She took off her high-heeled shoes and put on slippers from her handbag, then she removed her jacket and put on a long t-shirt that covered her skirt. She carefully placed her handbag and jacket on a small chair in the corner of the living room, near a huge window, and proceeded to start the wash. She was very careful with the towels, especially the whites. She completed the task and then hung them on the clothes line. The white towels glistened in the sunlight and Brenda looked at her handiwork and was pleased. Mrs Mortimer came out to look at the line, 'Oh they smell heavenly; I like that.'

Mrs Mortimer took Brenda inside and then told her that she would now be cleaning the upstairs and that she should begin with the bedrooms. There were five bedrooms and Mrs Mortimer showed her exactly the way she wanted the rooms. Brenda cleaned the rooms thoroughly. Mrs Mortimer examined the rooms with a white glove. She wiped her hands on the furniture and they were spotless. She smiled, 'You know Miss, I like that there is no dust. Ok, take the towels from the line now.'

When Brenda took the towels from the line she folded them neatly, while Mrs Mortimer watched. She picked up one of the towels; she smelled it, rubbed it on her cheeks, rubbed it on the back of her hand, gently moved it up and down her arm and then sighed. 'Yes, they are very soft, ok come back tomorrow.'

It was 7 p.m. and Brenda was bushed, but she was happy that Mrs Mortimer seemed pleased with her work. She went back the next day. Mrs Mortimer told her to start with the rooms that she did the day before as dust would have fallen on them overnight. Brenda did as she was told and completed all the tasks. Mrs Mortimer seemed satisfied. She told her to return for the final day. Brenda's tasks on the final day were to clean the living room windows and iron all of Dr Mortimer's clothes. As she washed the outside of the windows, she saw a Rastafarian, a mobile vendor across the road selling fruits and juice. He waved to her and she nodded in response. Mrs Mortimer looked out the window, shook her head and said nothing. Then Mrs Mortimer examined the clothes Brenda had ironed and hung in a closet. Mrs Mortimer scrutinized the clothes with a meticulous eye. She breathed deeply and then sighed. It was now the end of the day and Brenda was to be remunerated.

'Miss, I am not pleased you know. The clothes are not done properly, the windows are a mess, and everything is in disarray. I am so tired of you young girls coming here to work and not knowing how to do a God damn thing! You, you come here looking like a blasted high profile secretary, wiggling up your ass and showing off.' Then in a hushed tone Mrs Mortimer mumbled, 'This is same kind of thing that caused poor William to lose his way. God bless his soul. The heart attack intercepted the disgrace...' Mrs Mortimer stopped, then her decibel increased with annoyance and infuriation, 'You made a total mess of the house, and you sat down every time you thought I was not watching you. You did absolutely nothing and now expect me to pay you! Get out of my house! Lazy! Uncouth! Catapulting pirate! You cannot be paid because you did nothing that earned merit for the three days! You think I have money to waste Miss.'

'Please Mrs Mortimer, I did everything you told me to do and you said you were pleased. I need the money Mrs Mortimer, please!' Brenda cried.

'Come, come now, you must leave. I have nothing else to say to you.'

Mrs Mortimer escorted Brenda out of her house. She threw her handbag and belongings to her. Brenda could not get another word in. Although she had been trying to reason with Mrs Mortimer, she was just not allowing her to say anything. 'Get out of my yard I said, or I am going to call the police! Listen Miss, you get your comeuppance for the so-called work you claimed to complete.'

Brenda turned and looked at Mrs Mortimer, her eyes piercing with a stern stare.

'Hello lady, do not dare to look at me in that tone! Uncivilized! Who do you think you are? Coming in here behaving like you are somebody. I will have you know that my daughter is a lawyer and my son is a doctor, so don't you play with me child,' Mrs Mortimer scolded scornfully.

Slowly Brenda turned her head and stared deeply at Mrs Mortimer. 'Yuh daughta is a damn prostitute and yuh son is a blasted sissy!' she fired with rage. She walked the long corridor to the gate. She was engulfed with fury and frustration. She started heaping stones at the large gate. Brenda picked up a big rock and with her left hand, like a fast bowler in a serious cricket match, began hurling them onto Mrs Mortimer's house. Brenda was like the Incredible Hulk in his transforming phase.

'Yuh wicked wretch! Gimme mi money!' Brenda yelled as her profligate throwing of stones hit windows and grills, which amazingly never broke.

Mrs Mortimer was sitting on the veranda and she absconded to the inside, as the stones hailed down like a wicked storm on the house.

'Hey blood fire woman! Gimme mi money now!' screamed Brenda in a possessed voiced. The sound of the stones were inimical. The ammunition was running low. Brenda walked up to the grill and shouted, 'If I don't get my money now I gwey mash up yuh house, yuh rotten belly gal.'

Mrs Mortimer smelled the rat. She knew that this was no easy feat; she quickly tossed the money outside as she realised the blows had subsided only for a moment. 'Here – take your money vagabond! I do not ever want to see you again. Good Lord! You are crazy!' Mrs Mortimer hurried inside, locked her door, locked all the windows and drew all the curtains. She sat in the little corner chair near one of the windows in the living room and peered outside to make sure Brenda was gone.

Brenda was reloading and this time closer to the house. She picked up her money and counted to make sure it was all there. It was there and more. She folded the money and pushed it in her bra. She took her rag from her bag and wiped her tears. Taking off the slippers, she put on her high-heeled shoes, took off the t-shirt, put on her jacket, patted down her hair and breathed with relief. Indeed, she had exorcised the demon! Brenda turned and walked away briskly. As she closed the gate behind her, she saw the curtain from the window slowly drop down. The vendor climbed on a slope to get a balcony view of the vindicated inquest.

Brenda latched the gate and walked away quickly. She heard a voice trying to get her attention; it was the Rastafarian selling on the side of the road. His animated summons made Brenda motion toward him.

'Hey daughta, shake mi hand!' Brenda extended her hand with reluctance and uncertainty. 'Shake mi hand again, man.' Brenda did as requested. 'Hey, yuh know how many girls I had to give bus fare because dem work and di wicked woman refuse to pay them. When I saw you going in, I shake di I head and say another one boy, but daughta yuh surprise mi! Yuh look so gentle and fragile. Bwoy I would neva tink a daughta like you woulda deal so wicked. Yuh get yuh money?'

Brenda nodded in the affirmative and started to walk away.

'Shake mi hand again. See a jelly here, cool down yuhself, hold a drink, on me.'

ONE AN DRIVE
Jodianna R Clarke

WAS THIS HIS final blow? Was this my undoing? Everything went black as his fist lodged beneath my ribcage and he released my neck from the gallows of his left hand. I clung to the door for support as I gasped for breath … a long breath that felt like my last before I collapsed onto the hard wooden floors. Wooden floors were something we had in common. We had both been sent off to separate boarding schools after Common Entrance, where wooden floors, timed meals, straight lines and tight schedules were our constant companions. Back then, going to boarding school was a normal thing for young children in our community. It was a badge of merit to our parents who prided themselves on earning the mighty US dollar and giving us a better life than they themselves had. When he had finally found me on Facebook we had spent minutes, hours, days, weeks, months reminiscing over the shared details of our childhood. Talking to him every day was like finding home again – a home that only people from our community could understand.

Hills. You had to go there to understand. The winding narrow roads where the air got cleaner and cleaner with the ascent. Where everyone knew everyone and everyone's business. Hills was a place where children walked to pre-school, primary school and high school – we just walked. We were in Jamaica, but Hills was different. We spoke differently and understood things that outsiders just did not understand, like 'Unda di tree a Charlton', and that the name of the community where I grew up was actually Happy News!

Through stories passed down from those before us, we knew that the slaves had escaped the coasts of Discovery Bay and Seville and had taken off into the hills spreading the happy news of freedom. What those slaves did not know was that we would forever be in the white man's grasp, despite their great and daring escape. The land they had settled on was invaluable, as below the surface of their farms and chicken coops was a precious commodity called bauxite. This commodity would see white men, loud noisy trucks and 'dust money' becoming staples of our little community and woven deeply into our childhood experience. Their constant presence explained the creaminess of his complexion and the fact that he always seemed to have money and nice things as a little boy. It also explained why after one Christmas holiday, around the time we were in Grade Nine, he just disappeared, and I heard he was gone to farrin. 'Him fadda file fi him chile,' was all his grandmother said to me when I went enquiring one third weekend when we should have both been home from boarding school.

We spent hours, days, weeks and months recalling how we had lost touch and his incessant search for me all those years since he migrated. I shared my wonderful journey as the bright church girl that did everything right, degrees from Northern Caribbean University on scholarship and a nice little job. I shared my opinions on the evolving role of women and our remarkable achievements since the days of our grandmothers. We clashed often over how different our views were: mine strong and independent, his fiercely traditional.

He took me on his journey of migration: as a fourteen-year-old he was suddenly uprooted from all he knew, only to learn the only help he was getting from his father was getting him into the country. He barely made it through their high school system and had learned to be a barber from another Jamaican guy in his building who had taken him under his wings. He had two barber shops of his own and was venturing into male hair products. It seemed we had made up for the fifteen years we had missed in a few months of conversation.

'Why u did give so much trouble bwoy?'

'No reason … l was just a troubled pickney.'

'U memba shoving me into Ms Blake cupboard roun de back a Grade Six?'

'Me did like you.'

'Like me? No sah … you only like the brown girls wid curly hair.'

'Me did like you me say.'

'You know mi granny march dung the hill to your granny house to tell her to control you.'

'She probably just laughed … she use to dat.'

'Me use to hear you give nuff headache too when you were boarding at St Paul's.'

'Fi true?'

'You change?'

'A bit.'

A cold chilling feeling coming from below my ribcage shocked me back to the present.

'Hey … hey are you ok?' he asked, in a deep twang that made him look and sound like the stranger that he was. I spoke no words as he held me up like a newborn baby and ran his hands over the cut his hand had caused while grabbing my neck.

'I have some gifts for you. Come, I have all the stuff you said you love.'

As he led me, like a father leading his child, I looked out the window of the villa we had rented in Negril for a week at the end of July. How could the outside world still be so beautiful, when inside I was raging? As we made our way to the bedroom I was greeted by a beautiful mahogany king bed and a ceiling high full-length mirror with huge glass double doors that swung out to a pathway leading to the turquoise water of the Caribbean Sea. The curtains with their tropical theme beautifully framed the outside with dancing seagulls beckoning me to come outside and play. I planted myself slowly on the bed in response to the throbbing pain that was now shooting between my head and side with no direction as to where to make its landing.

With a Santa-like smile, he lifted a suitcase to the bed and beamed with pride. 'This is all for you.' He began the grand unveiling. Pairs of shoes – Nike sneakers, Jessica Simpson stilettos and Crocs in every colour. Jackets and shirts – casual and super stylish with dresses for work and church. Then came the perfumes – *The One* by Calvin Klein, *Sauvage* by Dior and Gucci *Guilty*.

'Happy?'

A nod.

'Love them?'

A smile from my cheeks.

He then reached into his pocket to reveal a beautiful rose gold bracelet engraved with the words 'Jemma and David'.

My breath was going again. You see, my bow-legged grandmother had taken on the task to raise me and had named me after the woman on the red pancake boxes that came in the barrel from my mother every year. She had big dreams for me to become something, and so before I even entered the world, my destiny was set, I would be Jemima Sarah Black.

'I love rose gold,' I said, with a smile from my cheeks and water filling my eyes. The pain below my rib cage was pounding from the blow. 'Thank you,' I mouthed, as the first tear ran down my face.

He reached out to wipe the tear. The roughness of his fingers against my face was like my grandmother using Scotch Brite to wash the soup pot outside on Friday before Sabbath. Rough and coarse.

From what felt like my glass prison, with a pain rocking my side, I could see the sun setting in Negril. Hues of orange and yellow were all dancing together to form the perfect montage of colour with the blues of the shoreline receding in response to the sun bidding goodbye. Everything around me was picture perfect. The villa was stunning, the sunset was perfect. Before me lay gifts every girl would dream of. Only a swollen face, a bleeding neck and what felt like a sword stuck in my side was spoiling this scene.

'Our reservations for dinner are for 8 pm at that restaurant you recommended – Starlight Chateau. I wanted to catch the sunset, but we can catch it tomorrow,' he said looking up from his phone.

Just yesterday, I found that accent sweet ... yesterday I had dreams of what today would be like. The meeting at the airport earlier this morning was awesome. I departed my Knutsford Express bus with dreams of falling asleep under the Negril stars and making selfie videos in front of champagne sunsets. The greeting was that of two long lost friends, reunited at last. With patty and jerk chicken as his first food requests, we spent some time in Montego Bay soaking up each other's company and some good Jamaican food. It was as if time stood still and no one else existed as he animatedly shared about the last time he came to Jamaica for vacation. After three hours of enjoying the second city, we took our rented Belta further westward and so our glorious week of exploring the island was about to begin.

But something changed as we drove; slowly the laughter-filled conversations that had flowed so easy for weeks on end had become difficult as we sped through Sandy Bay. From disagreeing on the pace of his driving to arguing about the exact location of the venues we had agreed to visit, my need for structure and a plan was crashing against his need for speed and adventure. As the car dipped into Mosquito Cove the insults flew and rang out through the air. 'Yu too uptight man … Relax!' he chided.

'Put on yu seatbelt and enjoy the ride.'

'No tell me fi relax,' I snarled back with claws out ready for a fight.

Then came Ms Lucea. Oh Ms Lucea with her narrow roads and sharp corners only making matters worse. We crawled to a standstill, as navigating the constant flow of pedestrians and sidewalk vendors in the small town of Lucea was no easy feat. In response to the deafening silence that had joined as a passenger, I slid my headphones in my ear to spend a little time with my favorite artiste Chronixx.

'What you doing?'

'Listening to likkle Chronixx.'

'So I flew all dis way for you to tune me out? I left my businesses for somebody else to run for you to complain about my driving and then tune me out!'

'Me neva beg you fi come a Jamaica, you offered. I need no man to take me anywhere and do a thing for me so no badda wid dat speech.'

I was soon to learn that the liberation of the Jamaican woman was the right of a select group but me, Jemima Sarah Black of Hills, St Ann with the thermometer I had growing behind my name had signed mine away. No sooner had I carried my own bags up the staircase of the brightly coloured villa we had rented for the week than my declaration of independence was revoked. With a grab of my neck and a punch in my side, he took me completely by surprise. No discussion, no debate, my independence was revoked. This happened to other women but not to me. I was smart. I was educated. I did not depend on a man for anything. My bow-legged, brown-eyed grandmother called me Princess. I did not play with the other kids in the community; I was better than them. I never mixed nor mingled with certain 'bwoys', I was too good for that. I was not a 'cayliss, wutliss gyal'. This did not happen to me. I felt the tectonic plates beneath me shift.

Again the pain yanked me into the present, as he went to take a call in the other bedroom; I slowly slid off the mahogany bed and made my way to the mirror. I was now face to face with the damage; I looked better than I felt. Other than stain marks from my make-up running down my face, I looked normal. What felt like a slit to my throat and a sword protruding from my side was only a small cut on my neck and black and blue spots on my face.

But was that me?

I couldn't make out the eyes staring back at me in the mirror. 'Jem.' I reached out to touch my image in the mirror. 'Jemma,' I whispered to myself as if trying to wake myself up from a bad dream.

'We have dinner at eight.' His coarse voice shattering my solitude.

It is a miracle what a hot water rag, some Advil, foundation and contour, pencils and lipsticks can do. I re-approached the mirror after what felt like minor surgery, putting myself back together and I was beautiful again, but the light in my eyes was turned off. I ventured out through the double doors to take in the vastness of the darkened Negril shoreline and to use its calmness to still the wind that was howling in my soul. The creaking of the bedroom door pulled my attention away from my meditation and there he was – emerging in a crisp white button-up shirt and sea foam blue pants – a sharp contrast to my midnight black shorts romper and blood red Bridgette sandals. He held up his hand to show me that he too had a bracelet with our names engraved.

'You look amazing' he said, with that boyish grin I used to love back in primary school. 'Let me put on your bracelet.'

'Thank you,' I replied, as I held my hand out.

As our Belta pulled away from our villa I took special notice of where I was. Our villa was three villas down from the left turn, and around the corner from the main gate. I took note of the walk-in gate at the security post and the fact that persons were gathered there, apparently waiting for taxis. Good.

'When was the last time you come Negril?'

I felt the coarseness of his hand on my thigh. The memories of teenage joy were peeping from around the corner. 'After my school graduation, my English Teacher Ms Williams carried us on a half island tour to Negril. She took us to Jungle night club!'

The sound of laughter filled the air we shared. The kind of laughter that erupted from your belly and brought tears to your eyes.

'Waaaaaa ... your Christian teacher bruk unnu out!'

'Mi sey.'

'How unnu get inna di club?'

'Me no know, but we get eeen. If me poor granny ever know, she start fast and pray same time.'

The conversation continued along the road, to our boarding school days filled with terrible housemothers, third weekends and tuck boxes. It was about a half an hour drive to what seemed to be Negril town, as my eyes drifted to the time on the car radio. Good. We started the winding road with the moon seemingly beckoning us to come and sit. With a slight ascent the road got narrower and narrower with tall wooden gates hiding what I assumed were the million-dollar seaside investments.

'Quiet angel,' with a squeeze to my thigh.

A smile from my cheeks. 'Taking it in and hungry,' I chuckled.

As we emerged from the car and began making our way to the hostess desk my breath was taken away for the second time today, but now it was by the view. The view was majestic. Only in Jamaica could the beauty of the night rival the beauty of the day. Where stars dance across the sky with their shadow lighting the ocean beneath, as if moving to a live band playing sweet reggae music. It was as if the moon was staring right at me and at any minute would put out her hand and say 'Welcome'. Our hostess greeted us warmly, and we were seated on the edge of the patio where the moon was my next-door-neighbour and the waves were like children fighting over toys downstairs.

'This menu bad!' I exclaimed loudly, admiring the menu back and front. 'Shrimp, lobster, scallops, mussels and lots of fish options.' My kind of place – I was ecstatic!

'Nothing for me though. This is your kinda place, uptown fancy food,' he groaned. 'No pork, no curry goat.'

'Uptown?' I chuckled. 'Not at all. Likkle country girl from Hills.'

'Yu no act like a country girl, with all those fancy degrees and big words. You're all about you and see you choose a restaurant with only food you like!'

I sat in silence.

'Yu always inna yu head, always have an answer to everything,' he said with a look of disgust. 'I like my ooman dem calm, quiet and just listen to me. You do not need all that, I will take care of you.' With a hiss of his teeth he started staring me dead in the eye. 'I'll give yu money, anything yu need but me cyah tek di "betta than yu" behaviour. A so yu granny grow yu enno. Yu couldn't even ramp wid we when we were kids ... as if yu a smaddie.'

I saw the moon beside us get smaller and the waves below us get louder. The stars that were dancing to sweet reggae music had all stopped as if waiting on a response. A response I had not given all day as my well-done face hit the board floor. A response I had not bothered to share as I was gasping for air with my feet dangling from the ground. I had smiled at the gifts and the compliments and used make-up to hide the cut around my neck. I had used Advil to numb the pain in my side. The moon had retreated but the stars were waiting. My grandmother who had spoiled me rotten and built me up from the broken pieces she had been given, was waiting. The women before me who had fought and toiled so I could have even got a basic education as a nappy head black country girl, were waiting. My daughter that I dreamed of having one day was waiting on me to respond. As I got up and shoved the perfectly set table into his bulging chest, the shattering of glass and the clinking sound of falling cutlery provided the perfect backdrop to the volcano that had erupted inside me. With tears like hot lava running down my face, I screamed, 'No chat bout mi granny!'

I raced through the restaurant to the hostess desk. 'I need a taxi!'

With a puzzled look she pointed me to the gate where other staff were waiting at the end of their shift. As a taxi pulled up all six of us crammed in and I whispered to the guy sitting next to me that I needed to get to Montego Bay. He explained that the taxi would be passing the night bus stop and I could get transport from there to Lucea and then to Montego Bay.

I took stock of what I had on me. My purse with two thousand dollars, my phone and charger, a lip gloss and my NCB bank

Island Voices

card were all tucked in my little dinner bag. As I exited the taxi and stood in Negril, my insides were erupting in anger, fear and anxiety. I was reclaiming my freedom even if it meant travelling in the dead of night. Women before me had done it; they had run through cane fields and waded across rivers just to get to freedom. A woman's freedom was everything!

As I waited for what felt like eternity, I heard it! Cutting through the noise of competing speakers that were keeping the town alive. Riding on their waves like a chariot coming to rescue me.

It was my call to call to freedom! Never before had I been so grateful to hear these words.

'Lucea ... Lucea ... Lucea!'

'One an Drive!'

MOUNT SHEOL PRIVATE HOSPITAL
Geon Codd

TODAY WAS SUPPOSED to be our anniversary, Antoine's and mine. And yet, here I am from my watchtower munching on these stale palets de dames all alone instead; mourning not one loss but two: the love of my life, and my first patient to 'die'.

Coincidence, perhaps? Or the twisted gestures of a sadistic demiurge. My punishment, every July 15th, I'd be remembering souls prematurely departed from the realm of the living.

From my watchtower on the second storey, a bench in the skyway between two of the buildings among the total triad of structures, I could observe a great deal of the hospital's premises.

That pale woman in the antiquated garments knelt often on the verge of the pond. And though the day was swelteringly hot, she neither fainted from exhaustion under her habiliment, nor even seemed bothered in the slightest by said convolution of clothing—not to my surprise I suppose.

That day, five years ago, had started out exactly like this one, sunny and bright. And yet, as I look out in the distance, I can see storm clouds approaching. Of course, the sadist that he is, God would set the stage again today, replicate that haunting July 15th setting for me once more.

We were in our final year of college, and we had just got out for summer break. My fiancé, Antoine had planned a week for us out in Yvoire, a quaint little medieval town in Rhone-Alpes. This little getaway served a two-fold purpose: the first, to provide us with a much-needed break, our last semester was an arduous one; the second purpose, a sort of celebration that we had been engaged for a year.

I was eagerly looking forward to this sojourn. Why, we'd have picnics, and probably drive around until we found something interesting to do. Perhaps I would get thrilled seeing some antique store on the corner of only God knows what street. Maybe I'd demand Antoine to stop the vehicle so I can quickly hop out and pet a cute dog walking on the roadside. I'd smell some flowers or something, anything really; I excited quite easily anytime I was with Antoine.

That day started out warm, fresh and sunny; a truly beautiful day the likes of which I hadn't seen yet that year's summer. Perhaps, it was a day too beautiful, for shortly after we had embarked on our drive—one that would take us hours to get to our final destination—the sky turned dark.

For a time, we kept on driving, ignoring the rain, assuming it would have stopped as quickly as it had started ... It didn't however, but only intensified.

I insisted that we turn back or stop at some diner, surely arriving an hour or so later wouldn't cost our week much; but Antoine, mon amour, he could be stubborn sometimes.

The rain had matured into a full-on storm now. A storm in the middle of July.

The lightning was an intense lead, putting on a striking performance, illuminating the areas around us. But the thunder was no less a seasoned performer, never skipping a beat, following diligently in the shadow of the spotlight the lightning had stolen, nay, manufactured for itself, moments earlier.

I begged Antoine to at least pull over to the side of the road, and weather out the storm. I had packed more than enough snacks for our drive anyway. It seems they were to come in handy, as this storm appeared to not being quelled any time soon.

But, of course, Antoine insisted we go on. 'Don't worry, Angelien, darling, I'm an excellent driver,' he assured me, 'you've got nothing to worry about!'

Of course, I knew he was an excellent driver, but I could not assume that of every other driver on the road ... I should have knocked on wood thrice, or quickly made a sign of the cross at that thought, then maybe I wouldn't have jinxed us.

As we drove a bit further down that Autoroute du Soleil, the storm grew to its strongest. 'I think, I very well should pull over now, cygne,' Antoine said to me, 'the storm's getting too much.'

'Oui, mon amour, you should,' I quickly agreed.

Up ahead, I could see a light making its way through the rain towards us.

Antoine bent his neck forward and squinted his eyes to find a suitable place along the motorway where we could park.

The light drew closer to us at great speed.

The driver was on the wrong side of the road, somehow, he had made his way into our lane.

'Tony, Antoine, darling, quickly get to the side.'

'Cygne, I can't park over there, that's a—'

I briefly made out the silhouette of the cab of the 18-wheeler truck before the light from its high beams began flooding into our little Volkswagen Beetle.

I gasped, 'TONY! GET TO THE—!'

'BANG!'

The force of the impact made my body jolt; my neck would spend the following weeks in a collar due to the whiplash. If only my beloved had been afforded that same privilege.

Our car was launched backwards into a ditch.

For a time afterwards I simply sat there in silence in that passenger seat … hardly thinking much—well, if anything at all, really. I just sat. It hadn't been a voluntary thing either; the thought 'I will sit here in silence' had never crossed my mind. Furthermore, I don't recall it ever occurring to me to make a phone call, or to get out of the car, or examine what the warm liquid running down my legs was … or to look to my left.

But eventually, I did, I did look to my left. At first, I just—I just stared at him, placidly, apathetically.

His neck was bent unnaturally, and his face was all bloodied—punctured with broken glass.

But it soon occurred to me to—well, to do the only thing I felt I could do in that moment, really.

I screamed. At the top of my lungs, I screamed. I wept bitterly, and kept shouting his name amongst it all.

I had thought him dead, but no, he was still dying, for he suddenly coughed up blood as he began to wheeze and struggle to breathe: wearily, painfully.

I forced the passenger side door open, but I could hardly move. My legs had been caught up somewhere there among it all.

But I could hear my Antoine's breaths getting deeper, and the time in between them getting longer, and he began coughing up even more blood; and I was now afraid he would begin to drown on it.

So, with every bit of strength I could muster, and still high on adrenaline, I dragged myself out of the passenger's side—leaving some of my flesh and stockings behind. I limped around to the driver's side of the vehicle, somehow managed to yank the door open, and pulled my beloved out.

I soon realised his throat had been slashed. Blood trickled from it like a spring.

I sat in the mud, with my love's head resting in my lap.

But my world soon began to spin as it likewise darkened.

When I awoke, I found myself in a hospital room—Room 113 actually, just down a hallway from here in the dormitory sector of this damned hospital. I asked for my Antoine, only to be informed that he was dead. He had flatlined just before the ambulance drove in here through those Victorian gates outside.

I had narrowly escaped the same fate—the doctors couldn't stop reminding me over the weeks I spent in recovery.

And afterwards, though my physical wounds were healed, for a long time, the emotional wounds were festering; raw and inflamed. But the things I have seen during my tenure here at this hospital have led me to the conjecture: that death may not be the end, nor even a stepping-off point from which we journey to our maker.

And so, I was zealous to complete my studies, and after procuring my degree, and passing the National Licensure Exam, I was eager to begin my work.

I came here specifically, hoping that I could see Antoine once more.

I haven't yet. Perhaps, he is hiding from me.

I gazed outside. The woman knelt there, like a statue of marble, pale and motionless.

A boy skipped up to this woman out of time. He squatted beside her and stretched his arm out to place something in the pond—something small—something white.

I stretched out my neck and squinted my eyes to get a better view.

The woman's head turned slowly—turned unnaturally—to look at the boy.

She soon positioned herself frontally. Opening her arms cautiously, she planned to ensnare—no, *envelope* the boy ... her intentions had changed promptly.

But another woman soon came running from out of view towards them.

She was frantic. She shortly scolded the boy.

He hung his head in embarrassment at the reprimanding.

The two soon walked away, the woman holding the boy tightly, lovingly by the hand.

Little Miss Victorian Era, however, was left with her hands outstretched, yearning for the boy.

After a while, she retired to her initial, signature, kneeling-pose overlooking the pond.

That thing soon floated by her—Ah, yes, I see it better now! A boat—a boat made of paper was what the boy had placed in the pond.

But you see, things had played out differently for the boy and the reprimanding woman. For through their eyes, there was only, well, *themselves* at that pond. No extra woman, outdated and sombre, reaching out to embrace some wandering and spirited boy.

No. They had not seen nor heard, nor smelled that woman there. The only appeal to their senses was perhaps a chill which ran down their spines as they neared her, their hair standing on end, their skins turning to braille, but perhaps attributing it to some sudden gust of wind, shrugged it off as insignificant.

However, to Victoria there, those two were as real to her as that placid pond whose verge she knelt at, the summer sun above heating the day, and the calico clothing engulfing her.

To Victoria there, those two were as alive and very much a part of the world as she was.

She reached out with a hand towards the boat drifting slowly by her … her hand passed through it.

Someone sat cautiously next to me on the bench.

A chill ran down my spine, my hair stood on end as my own skin turned to braille.

'E-Excuse me, miss.' A young boy's voice addressed me timidly.

By his voice alone, without having to turn to look at him, I know who he is ... was.

I had grown attached to the keeper of that voice too much for my own good.

Attachment, in this line of work, a thing equally as discouraged as much as it is endorsed. A contradicting thing attachment is for a caregiver.

But one can only grow attached to a patient whose sufferings you soon realise have not been justified. You see them fight day in, and day out, as they try so desperately to hold on, refusing to succumb to their afflictions ... But 'God only picks the most beautiful flowers', no? Even if they were still young, not even fully-bloomed, with a whole life before them to be lived, and yet ... And yet for them to die in such a—such a drawn-out and demoralising way.

Hmm, some 'god' he is.

'Miss, uh, I-I'm sorry to bother you, but—' I think he made an attempt to grab at my sleeve, for my sleeve fluttered briefly and the skin on my upper arm grew colder, 'Do you know where I am? I—I can't seem to remember much—I—'

I ignored the boy. Though it pained my heart, I ignored the boy. Best not to give him any ideas that he was still *really* here amongst the living, perhaps that is how he could pass on.

'Can you not hear me as well, miss?'

I shivered, 'Whoo, there's a draught in here,' I commented.

'Miss, if you can hear me, please resp—'

I stood up abruptly before the boy could finish.

'I need to get a sweater.' I thought aloud as I hurried away. These grounds had ensnared yet another prisoner.

Yes, so is the fate of those who perish here at Mount Sheol Private Hospital.

'Sheol': 'grave', 'abode of the dead', morbid, but fitting name for a grounds of its ... calibre. But I suppose whoever named the hospital hadn't a choice in the matter; the locals had already come to know the hill it resided upon as being a depository for the dead. For its reputation and name had long preceded whomever—only just recently in its wearisome history—decided to construct the three grandiose buildings on its turfs. But then afterwards, to so ostentatiously advertise the facility as one of 'the most cutting-edge', 'most avant-garde' private hospitals in—if not only France—hell, all of Europe, most naturally ... the sheer arrogance I tell you.

And yet, we could not save the life of one child. But maybe 'It was his time', yes?

Truly, I would have liked if he was 'in a better place'.

Regardless, a true depository for the dead this hospital was, as caricatures from its extensive, traumatic ... haunting history really, remained, lingered between our land of the living and their dimension for the dead; denying the fact of their demise to hold on to the hopes of the living.

As I made my way through the visiting area, sure enough, *he* was there, at his table next to the window: the bloodied soldier in the American WWII uniform; maybe the cause of many of the visitors' complaints of a 'draught' near that south-facing window.

Further along my walk, the bent-necked man hovered past me. I made sure not to look up at him, the sight of his starved legs and bony feet hovering just above the ground were enough to make me cringe.

As I turned into the elevator, I heard the whispers of the invisible lady, often giving passers-by the time of day.

And yet, after having seen, heard, felt the presence of all these ... personalities, for the entire year I've worked on these grounds ... I haven't caught the slightest glimpse of my Antoine.

SHE WORE RED TO THE CREMATION

Stephanie Ramlogan

SUCHITRA WORE RED to the cremation. She buttoned up a crimson blouse and outlined her lips in carmine, defiant with a type of joy at her uncle's passing. She went dressed like the fire that would finally claim what was left of him, revelling in his death.

To no one's surprise the funeral was small. Baal was not popular by any means. He had no hobbies beyond TV-watching, and barely drank any alcohol, so the friendships made at the local watering hole did not include him. He was just quiet some would say, while others considered him a hermit. A couple of co-workers from the factory came. A handful of family was there too, dressed in traditional white kurtas and head scarves, huddling a fair distance from the burning pyre, as thick black smoke pushed upward through the midday heat. The wood crackled loudly, pelting glowing pieces as it broke. People stared at the woman in red, no doubt whispering about her disrespectful funeral attire. But after all her years of silence over what her uncle had done, this was her only semblance of retribution, and she found satisfaction in their gossip.

She was raised to care a lot about what people say. This obsession with appearances was a cultural plague. People from Chatoo village tended to stay close to home, and everyone knew everyone. Children lived with their parents until they were married, and then their parents lived with them until they died. On a loop, this was their lifestyle. But not for Suchitra.

Her mother died giving birth to her. Her father was a fish out of water with this squirming infant, who cried incessant searching shrieks for the mother's milk he could not provide. Her cries stirred a madness in him. A cocktail of grief and regret drove him once to almost drown her in the kitchen sink when she would not stop screaming.

He was not meant to parent alone, he thought. Fatherhood was an accompaniment to mothering, and without a woman to care for the child in tender ways, who would jump to quell the baby's every gurgle, he was just a man with a motherless child. He felt no connection to Suchitra without his wife there, so he gave her to his sister when the baby was just over a week old, and then disappeared thanklessly into the city. Maya and her husband Baal had to accept that the child was their responsibility now, and did their best to scrub the stain of her brother's scandal out of the scornful village chatter.

When the pyre flames subsided, ash blew across the ground in swirls. Maya waded in the smoke saying the last thank-yous and goodbyes to Baal's former co-workers. A few family members were heading to her house. One cousin stood impatiently in the parking lot, leaning against his dusty Toyota Corolla, waiting for Maya to ride with them. The old woman wished the day could just end right then and there. She had dragged herself through a torturous eulogy, where Baal's boss, the closest person he had to a friend of any kind, spoke superficial things about the deceased like how punctual he was at the factory. The pundit repeated the same old passages about reincarnation and the cycle of life.

The day was more dull than it was depressing, she thought. Baal went out with a deserved lacklustre celebration for his punishable existence. His quietness was not humility, nor was it introversion. No, Baal was not a shy person. In fact, he was too brave. He was too bold and pushed himself in places he was not welcome. He kept to himself to evade suspicion, playing up the idea that if he were out of sight, he would be out of mind.

Suchitra was sitting in the concrete gazebo that families could rent for fancier funerals than this one was. She sat on the floor of it, with her legs hanging off the edge swinging. Her floral skirt was hiked up above her knees, bunched together and tucked between her thighs. It had been over thirty years since Baal first raped her, but she could still smell the musk of his wet neck and remember the bristle of his moustache on her cheek. She could still hear him too, those gruff exhalations when he finished himself on her belly. The mornings after, he acted like he did not even notice her presence. He would not look up from his newspaper when she entered the kitchen. He barely spoke to her at all for her entire life. It was only when he crept into her bed at night that she ever saw him exert any emotion at all. Baal was a brick wall of a person. Unaffectionate, unambitious and unexpectedly this child's rapist. On this gazebo floor she sat fidgety, sucking on the last inch of a cigarette, contemplating if she would go to the house out of respect for Maya. Just then, her aunt spotted her and made her way over.

'You would come by we later?'

'I can come if you want,' Suchitra replied curtly, flicking the cigarette into a drain, avoiding eye contact.

'Yeah. Come nah. When everybody leave, I have something for you.' Maya turned around before Suchitra could protest and headed towards the Corolla.

***

Suchitra only stepped into the yard when she saw the last guest drive away. She scrutinised the house. It was stuck in time, virtually unchanged since she had moved out on her wedding day. Older coats of aqua green paint peeped out from under flaked ones. Even the lone mango tree in the front yard had not grown any taller. Wrapped around a post which held up the garage galvanise, still hung the rusted chain that used to tie the family's mongrel who ran away and was never replaced.

Suchitra was married off to a boy that Maya and the pundit chose for her. They were both too young and too ill-prepared for marriage, but his parents were quite religious, and they were looking to have him settle down with a nice Hindu girl from the village who could help out around their house.

Maya slept in Suchitra's bed for six years before this, protecting her from Baal's intrusion, but she knew that the only way to guarantee the girl's safety was to get her out of that house completely. When Suchitra was about eleven, Maya woke up in the middle of the night to use the bathroom and noticed Baal was not beside her in the bed. She went looking for him. He was not in the living room, nor was he in the kitchen. But his car was in the garage so he had to be home. Her mouth filled with water, and her head with depraved thoughts.

Suchitra's door was shut, but Maya did not have to open it to confirm that Baal was in there. She pressed her ear to it and could hear him breathing heavily and grunting like he did when he climbed on top of her. She knew the sickening sound well. Even when she heard the girl cry, 'Please, I don't want to,' followed by the backhand of a slap, she did not go in. She was too embarrassed and afraid of what the next steps would be. *What would people say about them when they found out?*

She tearfully crept back into her bed where she lay on her side, wide awake contemplating the right thing to do. Baal slipped in beside her after only a few minutes, smelling of sweat and semen and contentedly fell right asleep.

From then, his frequent midnight disappearances no longer went unnoticed since Maya could not rest soundly anymore.

Within the week he had snuck out three times. Perhaps she should have confronted him, but Maya imagined that scenario to result in another type of nightmare all together. He would put them out into the road. Maya didn't work. How would she mind the child, far less herself? And who would ever want to help them, knowing that the girl was with a big man, and that Maya was put out? The best she could think was to ensure there would be no more of Baal's late night escapes, and she made different excuses to sleep next to Suchitra each night from then on. She would say that either Baal was snoring too much, or it was too hot in their room. Finally, when her diabetes was confirmed by the doctor, she said it was because she needed to be closer to the toilet at night. Baal never questioned her.

'You tell me to come for something,' Suchitra said impatiently. She had decided the moment that she walked through the front door that she actually did not want to be in that house. The weight of old oil and curry clung on the air like it always did. She fingered for a fresh cigarette and her lighter, before putting her handbag down.

'This wouldn't take long,' Maya assured her, sensing her anxiousness. She gestured to the doily-covered couch, holding a little black book. They both sat on opposite sides of the tiny living room facing one another. Maya slid her thumb along the ends of the book's pages, searching for a particular spot.

'Here it is.'

'What is this?' Suchitra grimaced, as she unfolded a cheque that was wedged between the book's gilded paper.

'Your uncle wanted me to give this to you,' she lied, 'like an inheritance.'

The truth was that while he was fading away at the hospital, Baal and Maya were working on his will together. When she asked him about leaving something to Suchitra, he sucked his teeth sharply and coughed, 'She is not my child. What she have to do with this?'

The cheque was for twenty thousand dollars. It was all of Baal's savings, and he had intended it only for his wife. Suchitra's face contorted into a tighter scowl, gripping the cheque trembling as she tried to find the word for what she was feeling.

Many feelings can only be released when you have the words to describe them. Until you can name them, you are trapped. This was one of those experiences that lacked its own vocabulary.

Suchitra stared at the cheque and the curves of her name written in someone else's hand. Her chest flashed hot and cold. She was facing a spectre. She had seldom been in her uncle's presence since the day she left home. She thought there was an unspoken understanding between them, that she would never have to bear more of him in any way.

When she was able to speak again she said, 'I don't want it.'

Maya's guilt was ringing in her ears. Nervously she kept wiping her slicked back hair with her hands, smoothing it over and over again. She had never told Suchitra that she knew what Baal had done. The confession stuck in her throat several times, washed back down with the guilt of not standing up to Baal herself. She never gave Suchitra the chance to unburden this secret. Instead she made the load bigger and heavier for them both by keeping it to herself. She continued to be a servile wife to this manipulative man, while the faultless child felt tormented and alone. She rolled rotis for breakfast and washed his clothes day in and day out. She picked up his drawers off the floor and boiled water for his bath. Maya let him use her body.

Looking down at the cheque, Maya scorned herself for her cowardice, knowing the money was a weak attempt at any absolution.

'If is me you worryin 'bout, don't be. I good. He was saving that for you, long time.'

'I can't.'

'Just take it nah. *Please*.'

There was something about that 'please' that echoed. Suchitra studied Maya, and recognised the same nameless emotion she herself was feeling – an ambivalence towards a thing you both desperately need and furiously loathe.

Every wrinkle around the old woman's eyes deepened, framing a face imprisoned in remorse. She oozed a distinct empathy that one could only have if they related. Or if they were a part of it.

'You know,' Suchitra whispered, rising to her feet. 'Aunty, did you always know?'

Maya's voice cracked so no words could spill smoothly. Instead of speaking, all she could do was exhale a long throated wail of admission.

'I ... so ... sorry,' she sputtered eventually, intimidated by the magnitude of Suchitra now standing over her, her blood-red clothing glowing in the afternoon light. Maya held her head, nodding uncontrollably, while becoming ensconced in humiliating sobs.

'You even worse than he,' Suchitra sneered, before streaks of tears and snot fell from her eyes and nose, swiftly rubbed away with the back of her forearm. Her eyes darted across the house, back and forth, blurring it all into a pink haze. The betrayal was tangible. She felt the thick film of it coat her teeth and her tongue. She felt to spit it out right there on the carpet. There were so many times she wanted to tell her aunt what Baal was doing to her, but she was too concerned about the choice she would be asking her to make. She didn't want to make *Maya* uncomfortable, ha. Meanwhile 'discomfort' would have been a happy trade for herself, in exchange for lifelong self-loathing and wanting to die. *But Maya always knew.* The moment hung like a wet painting, leaking and dripping. Baal's ghost nonchalantly turned the newspaper page in the kitchen while these two women mourned their plundered freedom a few feet away.

Suchitra stood over Maya, repulsed by the sight of her selfish grief. Maya continued to cry and shake with an outpouring of apologies. Suchitra was numb to it. With one firm swipe of her thumb, she ignited her cigarette lighter. A tall yellow flame shot up, and she kissed the cheque to the tip of it, observing the darkening paper as it curled. Just when it became engulfed in fire, Suchitra flung it aimfully. It landed in her aunt's pleading, outstretched hands and caught on the coconut oiliness of her palms.

MEMORIES OF THE RIVER
Claudia Allen-Williams

THE BODY, IF you could still call it that, lay in a messy heap by the riverside. Sort of like when you use a sharp machete with its blade glistening in the sun after a good persistent, intentional sharpening and 'chamba chamba up' a piece of useless meat and then throw it on the ground, without any care or regard ... like you never ever did in real life.

His clothes were all part and parcel of the bits and pieces, black with mud and dirt, splashed all over with his blood, bones and sinews. The flies were everywhere, as you would expect them to be. Buzzing around and alighting on the grossly bloody pile ready to go to work to devour him into nothingness.

The police was on one side of the rope standing all unconcerned, just there trying to keep passersby from the village from kicking or raging at the pile of red blotchiness or chopping it up even finer. Sarge had said, 'Enough is enough, de man done dead already, how much more chopping these people need to do? Justice done serve already, no more no lef fe dem fe get.'

The other body, that of the little girl in the white lace dress, had already been taken to the morgue. Accompanied by the expected weeping and wailing and screaming that happened when children are harmed ... when their lives are ripped from the land of the living ... violently and mercilessly by some black-heart man who had no part nor lot with God.

At the morgue, the body was handled with the kind of quiet grace and mercy that children deserve, living or dead. Way more mercy than that black-heart man showed her, squeezing the life out of her so no one would know.

Once she was wrapped up and tagged, the undertaker gave her now catatonic mother one last look before quietly repeating the Prayer of St Francis and crossing himself over and over as if to erase his burden and that of the aggrieved mother. The child's mother was now stone cold quiet, resigned to having no more tears to cry, just vengeance, murder and destruction in her heart.

***

The day had dawned like any other in a place far away people tend to refer to as paradise. Little did I know that it was going to be the kind of day that you never forget. One that sits in your soul and never eases up. Squeezing the life out of you, a little at a time.

Except for my dream the night before, nothing had indicated to me that it would end this way. I dreamt that Mama went down by the gully and brought back a bunch of Gros Michel bananas, pretty like money, glistening yellow like the sun, except for one green finger on the top hand. She was so mad to see de one green finger she promptly took a knife and cut it off. As she cut into it, the banana stain ran red, like blood. Green and blood: two things that make dreams worrisome and frighten children, parents and grandparents, who shake their heads for the pain that is sure to come.

Except that I didn't share it, to avoid the worry and guessing that would inevitably ensue. We wouldn't be allowed to go to Mango Walk or go tearing through the apple grove right after dropping our school bags on the night stand by our beds. All fun would be drained out of the coming day if I had told them of my dream.

The thought of Miss Getty's math test today did not excite me as it usually did, nor did the possibility of spreading out the brand-new contents of my geometry set sent from Boston by my big sister Kate. I got no pleasure from the smoothness of the wood of my new ruler as I anticipated using it in front of all my jealous classmates. All because of the uneasiness that had lodged itself in the pit of my stomach, threatening to forcefully burst through my chest, out of my body where nobody could handle it.

The only thing I could think about was to pray it off quietly as we navigated the narrow path from our house towards the River Road. The fog lingered all around us. I imagined that the water would be seriously cold this morning when we would take our bath just before heading home from our last trip fetching water.

I shuddered at the thought of the cool night that was behind us. The window in our room had been foggy all evening. When the fog settles in Point Hill, it did just that – settle – in every corner and crevice of the house, the yard and the entire village until the sun came strolling over the mountain in all its brilliance. The one place where it always seemed to hang on for dear life was by the river. It made the early mornings so much creepier and untrustworthy.

We heard the screaming when we approached the bend by Mr Clarke's cane field. It sounded like hell had been unleashed on earth into somebody's immediate reality... and they weren't ready to handle it!

My hands suddenly went limp and my water bucket crashed to the ground with a loud clang, landing at my feet along with all the blood that had drained from my entire torso. My oldest brother, who was ahead of us, halted in his tracks, shielding us with his wide torso, his outstretched hands forbidding us to take another step. Grasping my hand he quickly pulled my youngest brother and me into the bushes as we all crouched in fear. He looked from one side of the path to the other, carefully scanning the area to see if he could identify any immediate danger.

That's when the second scream suddenly penetrated the thick morning fog. It sounded like it was coming from the river. Several other screams pierced the air as my little brother quivered and ducked further down into the clump of grasses. The sound of running feet and cries of 'murder!' filled the air around us.

Villagers began appearing from all sides of the trail, materialising like ghosts in the foggy darkness of the morning. We became caught up in the urgency to run with everyone else towards the river, our buckets abandoned on the side of the trail. Something more immediate was happening, and we ran with the villagers towards the screams and shouts of 'murder!'

As we got to the clearing at the overlook we could see the river, calm and serene in its greyness, undisturbed except for a small white bundle floating on the surface towards the northern shore. People began appearing from nowhere, or so it seemed! Anger disturbed the early morning coolness of the river as the women wailed and the men grunted and shouted for vengeance.

A few men had waded into the shallows as others swam towards what now looked like the body of a little girl floating in a white dress. The crowd was gasping and pointing towards the river's surface. They brought the fragile bundle to the riverbank and set it down among the reeds by the clearing near where we stood.

I was afraid to look, but I peeked from one eye. I couldn't see her face but I could clearly see the pattern of lace on her clothes. I knew that dress well ... it was Sharla's, my seatmate in class. She had worn it on many occasions when I went to her house to play dandy shandy and dress up with her. As the crowd grew by the riverside that morning I knew this was it: My dream had now materialised into someone else's immense tragedy.

A murmur went through the crowd as I heard the name 'Kayudeh' repeated with a kind of rage that made my stomach muscles tremble. As the name reverberated through the crowd I knew instantly what it meant: justice would be swift and barbaric, like it usually is in these kinds of circumstances in the village. And it wouldn't be pretty ...

The men sprang into action with their shiny machetes in hand, heading towards the clump of pampas grass across the way, west of the river. They were now running hastily, peeling away from the gathered crowd with the kind of angry frenzy that in their minds the situation demanded. Shouts of 'Got him!' filled the air and the crowd seemed to drag itself towards the shouts. Two men emerged with a half-naked man in tow ... it was Kayudeh.

It was light enough for me to make out his bulging frame. His eyes were filled with fear as he strained against the ropes that the men had used to hastily bind his upper torso and to drag him to face the accusing screams. The crowd converged on him in an angry sweep. Someone yelled, 'Murderer!' and all hell broke loose!

My hand gripped the golden cross at my neck and I fell on my knees as the crowd pressed closer. I averted my eyes and looked up at the morning sky which was just beginning to clear, allowing the sun to peek through, its beams spreading across the sky and giving light to the chaotic and tragic scene below.

***

We were up real early that morning, racing to the river to fill the barrel to the brim before taking a bath by the river side and heading off to school. There was the usual clamour in the village as the roosters crowed and flapped around on their perches. The crickets had ceased their chirping and gone underground 'til later. All the cows and donkeys were waiting expectantly in their pasture as my Dada dressed quietly and deliberately, waiting for the kettle to squeal, letting him know his coffee was well on its way to the table with the fried dumplings and ackee and saltfish and corned pork. We knew Mama was in the kitchen as the clanking of the Dutch pots and pans signalled she was on the job. Mother Roz had already sent the daily coconut oil bottle, still warm from the heat of the fireside.

Dada didn't finish putting on his Constable uniform that day. At the sound of the piercing screams he ran half-dressed towards the river, his unbuttoned shirt flapping behind him, his sawed-off shotgun bouncing up and down on his shoulders. Everybody in the village knew when the screams of trouble came that he would be there. He got there just as the angry mob had completed their mission.

My brothers and I rushed towards him as he settled into the knowledge that he had been too late to make sure justice was served in its kindest form. He gathered us around him and did his best to walk us away from the bloody pile of tragedy and pain. We couldn't fetch water now, so he told us to go up to the community tank to get our water.

'Hurry up,' he said. 'Don't be late for school.'

That day at school was the worst. My math test was postponed, and the entire school was filled with a kind of sadness and grief that befitted the recent occurrences. Each class filed silently out for morning devotion at the Baptist church nearby, where the preacher and his staff from the Jamaica Baptist Union sought to comfort our hearts and souls with the words of the scripture. Our class in particular was petted and powdered as Sharla was a member of our class. Her empty seat was adorned with flowers fresh picked from her mother's garden and doused with oils and perfumes, all to cleanse and purify her innocent spirit as she entered Heaven.

Reverend Henry said, 'Children go straight to meet their Heavenly Father when they pass on, so the flowers and oils would make her ready to meet Him.' It was a relief to hear that after what had been done to her in her innocence.

The air of sadness and gloom that had settled in our class did not dissipate any when we returned from recess to find that Sharla's adorned seat had been removed into the foyer right under the wooden cross near the principal's office where it was carefully placed along with a photo of her flashing her beautiful megawatt smile.

Each of us stared gloomily at the framed photo as fear gripped my belly, pulling inwards. Miss Getty had us line up and pay our respects one by one to our dear classmate. As my turn came I pictured her soul rising up on the beams of bright sunlight piercing through the fog on the river, up, up above it all and into the arms of God.

There truly was evil in the hearts of men, as my mother sang in her songs sometimes:

There is evil in the hearts of men
Singer, you beware ...
Pray without ceasing ...
Lift your eyes to the Father!
There is evil in the hearts of men
Singer, you beware ...

BUSH TEA
Akhim Alexis

HER GARDEN WAS mobbed in green. It was so crowded that it strangled her small wooden house at the centre of the yard. From afar, it looked like a mini jungle, a quiet area of fenced land possessed by one woman, a familiar landmark resting at the bottom of St Catherine Hill. There at the bottom of the hill, flowers and fruits and weeds all coalesced into tangled architecture. But when observed from a closer vantage point, it all seemed logical, like she planned to hide in plain sight all along.

A narrow pathway from the gate to the front door lay bare as she stood at the top of her steps, like Moses parting the green sea of bougainvillea, mango, moringa and bay leaf. The image of her standing on her front porch with her battered engraved stick is what prompted the neighbours to call her Ms Moses, a title which she wholeheartedly embraced, causing her to never have a need to reveal her actual name. Her house balanced haphazardly on fourteen concrete bricks. It stood the test of torrential rains and vortex-like winds that threatened to uproot trees that stood firm against earthquakes and gnawing insects. At the front of the house stood four concrete stairs and a gallery, this was considered the waiting area for visitors and customers. She never allowed anyone inside, and no one could testify that they had ever seen beyond the black curtain which somehow refused to budge with the breeze.

Ms Moses prepared packs of her special medicine for the day's customers. You had to discuss your ailments with her in advance, she needed you to unpack every sickly detail. From the time you started feeling ill and just how many times you had to go to the washroom on that same day. She wanted to know if your husband did anything to aggravate you, and if you said no, she swore you must be lying, because 'the only time a husband does stop stressing out his wife is when he is dead.'

Although Ms Moses spoke about her family at length all the time, no one seemed to know her full story. They knew about her mother, but no elders ever actually saw her, because all their information came from the tongue of Ms Moses. She was the only historian of her lineage. And because of this communal ignorance, everyone joked that she was born a middle-aged woman with a headtie and no womb, she just walked out of her mother's vagina and told her mother to drink some mango-leaf tea to feel better.

The trust she garnered stemmed from generational tales. Tales she told to anyone she came in contact with, beginning with her mother's mother, blessed with the hand that heals. She claimed that she learned everything from her mother who worked alongside her grandmother, who was the assistant of a prominent Chinese doctor. 'Medical knowledge from the age of iron' was her marketing pitch to new reluctant customers. But there were always sceptics. She was a towering figure, piercings in all areas that you could think of, and her hair remained tied in a knot with a white cloth. Her bold discreteness caused naysayers to label her a scary madwoman, with nicer sceptics calling her a lucky mad scientist. The only man known to have loved her intimately had died in the attempted coup riots 20 years ago, and she still kept his picture over her bedroom cabinet.

***

One morning, as she was preparing to grind up spices, she heard a call out by the gate, 'Ms Moses, Good Mawnin.' She knew the voice, tough and tumble like a washing machine. Makah's voice was guttural, almost electronic, it could wake a sleeping rat from an underground pipe. Makah visited only to update her on neighbourhood gossip or to bring payments from customers who owe, but refuse to return to her house themselves, afraid she'll chastise them for holding out on payment. Despite their mutual friendliness, she never invited him in, so he waited on the bench near the front door.

She stepped outside and immediately noticed his fallen face. He looked jittery, like a man just found guilty of some heinous crime, waiting to be escorted to the guillotine.

'What's the problem, Makah? What have you shaken like disturbed earth?' she said.

Makah took off his hat and stood, 'Sickness is abound, Ms Moses. The talk is that it real deadly, no word if anyone in the village died yet, but I know somebody who catch it.'

Ms Moses was still standing, hands on her hip, head tilted to the sky.

'And what come with this sickness? Fever, vomiting?'

'Everything, Ma.'

'How you mean everything?'

'Ma ... fever, vomiting, headache, joint pain, even problems urinating. I heard that the boy who get it starting to lose his vision, he seeing blurry.'

'So is a young man then, hmm. In this village?'

'They don't want me to say, Ma, they 'fraid people scorn him.'

'Makah ...Who am I! Am I the common people or am I Ms Moses, leader, beginner and finisher?'

'Yes, Ma.'

'Bring him to me. Don't let the sickness spread before he reaches my doorstep, you hear me?'

'Yes, Ma.'

'Good, keep his journey under wraps, I don't need an audience, at least not now.'

'Yes, Ma.'

'Now what else is going on? You have any money for me?'

'Not yet. Susan say she still scraping up some coins for you, but she will bring it soon.'

'Soon is never soon enough! Don't make me have to slap on some interest, or worse yet, go and take back my medicine!'

'I'll tell her that, Ma.'

'Good. Now I'm going back inside, I have an athlete coming with an injured leg. His name is Jason. He will be a big runner when I am done with him, you watch.'

'I believe it, Ma.'

'Better believe.'

Makah tipped his hat and left Ms Moses posing on the front step. She had already begun concocting a mixture in her head, a new sickness meant a new opportunity for an experiment, and she needed something to boost morale, remind the people who she was.

No one in Kona Village knew the full name of any certified doctors, as they seldom visited the nearest hospital unless there were complications beyond the scope of the village doctors. A woman in labour went to the village midwife, who always called on Ms Moses for assistance. When the owner of the gas station got knocked down by a runaway car, Ms Moses visited him every day to administer care, pasting her thick blend of hibiscus leaves and steamed ochroes heavily mashed together with fig over his bruises. She accepted no complaints and answered very few questions.

***

The following Sunday, Makah came by with the sick boy in an old Datsun driven by a retired Taxi Man and instructed the driver to wait until they were ready to leave. The young man was clearly malnourished but heavy nonetheless, and Makah held the boy like a bag of hardened cement, close to his scrawny chest. Before he made it halfway through the yard, Ms Moses opened the door and started yelling instructions, 'pick some tomato leaf when you pass by that tree', 'don't drop the boy eh' and 'leave that bag down by the step.' She refused to meet Makah halfway, and already sweating herself, she kept dabbing a small towel under her arms as sweat trickled down the side of her breasts. The sun was clocking in overtime.

She had set up a small mattress next to the bench at the front door and told Makah to lay the boy on his side, back facing the sun. Despite being awake, with owl-eyes visible all the way from the car, the boy said nothing other than 'Hello, Ma' upon meeting Ms Moses, but she did not speak directly to him, a habit she developed over time to help distance herself from her patients, often speaking to their next of kin or whoever brought them to her.

She instructed Makah what to write and carry to his parents. 'First thing first, Makah, this boy is not eating right, look how he small—small like shrimp! Nobody who is starving could fight a sickness, let his people know he must eat, he needs protein,' she spoke to Makah without looking at him, focused on touching the boy's arms and legs, placing the back of her hand under his neck to feel his temperature. He was cold. This startled her somewhat, she never encountered someone who had felt so glacial in weather so humid, in fact, she had expected quite the opposite. Her fingers felt numb and she jerked her hand away from him as a reflex, then turned away and marched inside yelling, 'I'm coming back.'

Makah was confused said nothing, while looking down at the boy in worry.

Island Voices

She returned with a large teacup and the smell immediately soured the air. It was so pungent that it made the sick boy perk up and screw up his nose. The stray dog that spread himself out near the plum tree caught a whiff and scampered while making a crying sound, as though he was being chased with a stone. There were so many different aromas emanating from the cup that it was confusing to pin down what exactly Ms Moses put into the tea, but she held it with confidence. Makah knew better than to ask what was in the cup, as the smell made him nauseous and weak. 'That bush tea very strong, Ms Moses, I never smell anything like that before,' he said, with a reluctant tone. 'Yes,' she replied, 'strong brew for a strong sickness. I carefully concocted this bush tea, I always wanted to test it out. It's a vicious concoction of cayenne, tomato leaf, burnt hops, aloe-vera jelly and some other secret ingredients.' The young boy seemed unfazed by this list of items, but Makah's face made a left turn as he noted that she had not tasted the brew herself with a teaspoon like she usually does.

'You not going to taste it, Ma? To check if it's just right for him?' he said in a casual, almost passing tone.

'No, this is not for the healthy, it's for the very sick.'

Makah made no further remarks and assisted the boy in sitting upright, helping him hold the cup while he slowly drank the bush tea with steady encouragement from Ms. Moses.

※※※

It only took two days and one wearisome night for the boy to die in his mother's arms. He had drunk the bush tea every eight hours as instructed by Ms Moses, or so his mother said. The night of his death, he was in so much pain all he did was bawl. He wailed until the men living in houses down the street all came to see what was happening. Their wives were all praying together for his swift relief. He had been vomiting

blood and his gums were covered in sores, sores that only
arrived after his visit to Ms Moses. In fact, he had worsened
tremendously since drinking the bush tea. Ms Moses had
warned Makah that he will get worse before he got better,
and that they must stick to the routine, so his mother being
poor on options had obliged. When he took his last breath,
the first words of the grief-stricken mother was, 'Ms Moses!
That bitch. My boy! Oh, that woman killed my boy. Oh God
please why she had to do that, what it is she give my boy
to drink Lord. I never should have send him down by her
wretched house, I so sorry I give him that poison, please
bring him back God please.'

She bawled until dawn, then fell asleep, woke up and bawled
again.

Days before his death, as soon as the boy had left Ms Moses'
doorstep with Makah in the taxi, news had got out that she
had the cure for the new sickness, and an onslaught of sick
villagers who were previously hiding their illness, came for
bottles of the brew. Many had finished their 'every eight hours'
dose by the first day, drinking the tea like some sort of happy
juice, and their symptoms had gotten worse. One day after the
boy's death, three other villagers had died, all after drinking
the bush tea. Makah received all the complaints and warnings
firsthand. 'Tell Ms Moses her day is coming, we mourn now for
ours, but she will mourn for hers soon enough! Tell her she is
finished!' a coughing elder shouted.

Makah recited the threats verbatim, looking down on her as
she sat on the bench near her front door. 'You are finished, Ma,
they said that you are done,' he said.

She had missed the mark before, but never had it caused
such chaos, never had her healing caused the death of a client.
An echo of rumbling iguanas reverberated through her. Her eyes

Island Voices

were glassy, battling with the sun. She got up slowly, hand placed on the small of her back while she groaned with movement and looked at Makah with eyes blossoming water and said with conviction.

'I not finished until I decide, you hear me?'

'Ma, too much damage has been done, people dying because of that bush tea you hear?'

'People dying because they are sick, not because of my tea, and people die anyway, that's a factor of life.'

'How can you not feel a way, Ma? The boy has died! And if I must be real with you, whatever you put in that tea seemed to speed up that death. If you make a mistake, what is wrong in saying that? Everything can't go your way all of the time. I say you should close for a while and let things blow over, because right now nobody wants any guidance from you.' Makah had looked away from her immediately after uttering this, as he regretted his last statement.

'Who are you speaking to like that with all your chest?' she shouted. 'Me? You come to my house with that strong tongue to cancel my living? Listen here, I provide a service. Ms Moses did not hold anybody hostage and pour a beverage down their throat! But because things didn't work out, those backward people want to roll for me like thunder? Ha, hear me well, nobody but me could take me out! You hear me? Leave my yard now, boy!'

Makah refused to argue with her, the veins on her forehead were performing and her age started to show. He tilted his battered hat and turned to leave, before looking back one last time to say, 'I am no boy, Ms Moses, I am a big man with a wife and three children, all of who you never ask about. Working for you is the only job I've had for years, but you keep thinking about yourself, see where that takes you. Don't expect me to come back to work for you after today.'

He grabbed two low-hanging mangoes on his way out.

***

The sun had only just started to wake up by the time villagers started congregating to the front of her house the next day, and by sunrise, the narrow roadway was flooded with people. The birds who paid regular visits to the electrical wire floating above the roof were now circling the area in a frenzy, bothered by the restlessness below. Even people who were not infected by the sickness and never tasted the bush tea gathered and sang a remix of the holy spiritual 'Go Down Moses' on the spot:

Go down Ms Moses, Go down
Tryin' to make the mothers frown
She turn we whole world upside down
Let my people go!

The mother of the boy who was the first to die stood to the front of the exodus. Her husband along with a band of men stood gallantly with cutlasses and flambeaux, ready to be lit.

Ms Moses wrapped her head with a yellow cloth while glaring at the crowd outside of her kitchen window, careful not to open the curtain too wide thereby exposing her face. She was no fool, she had no intention of going outside to entertain an ambush, she would wait it out until they got tired or maybe assumed that she was not home. But at that moment, it entered her consciousness just how alone she was. There was no one she could call and the police would surely want to question her with regards to the death of the boy, which would undoubtedly cause a domino effect of doom. The only man she knew who could have protected her, had died in a gathering just as similar. This time, the coup was hers to endure. She stood in her dark kitchen and mouthed the words to the daunting chant which echoed through the walls of her leaf layered home:

Go down Ms Moses, Go down
Tryin' to make the mothers frown
She turn we whole world upside down
Let my people go.

A crack penetrated the singing, the avocado tree suffered the first blow. It took one chop to open the flood gates. The murder of Ms Moses' cherished jungle had begun. The angry mob successfully plundered her property, chopping trees and stomping on flowers, uprooting provision and stealing produce in buckets and bags. The pommerac and avocado tree fell majestically, troubling the wind and blessing the ground. Those who weren't focused on looting were steadfast on destroying, and through the slight opening in the window, a crestfallen Ms Moses with a drowned eye, looked directly at her once-close comrade, Makah, who was trying to hide near the outskirts but shouted the condemning chant, piling buckets of herbs and fruits in a wheelbarrow.

The blood boiled to the brim of her lips, she grabbed a knife from the kitchen and ran outside to the front step shouting 'Ungrateful bastards, stop this foolishness now! Leave my property alone. After all I have done for you, after everything? I'll cut each one of you one by one if you don't leave my territory now!'

But whatever retreat she assumed would occur as a result of her bold confrontation, did not happen. The first flambeau was lit by the mother of the sick boy. She flung the fiery bottle towards a towering mango tree, inciting a blaze that caught to branches and spread, rupturing the yard instantly.

Blinded by smoke and a sea of fire, Ms Moses dropped the knife and fumbled back inside, slamming the door. What did not escape in tears, slipped out in sweat, her face wet with shame and confusion. Was this how she would be remembered? Do they really want her to burn to ash together with everything else around her? And Makah, what could she have done differently to appease if not her clients, the only son she knew, a son now turned judge, jury and executioner? She knew the brew was strong. She knew if anything it would cause a jolt to the sick body, but she also knew the side effects, especially from mixing so many various items and adding an herb she had only used once before to numb the pain suffered by a recent amputee. It's what made her certain she did not want to taste it, as she assumed only a body on the edge of collapse should consume the tea, but in moderation. She figured it must be the lack of moderation that caused fatal reactions. There was no fury more potent than hers when she heard about the deaths. Her credibility and years of hard work were erased because of people's impatience for healing. She had heard that someone drank an entire bottle in four hours, collapsing by midnight. 'They never follow instructions,' she muttered to herself, as the glass window to the front of the house shattered from smattering flames.

There was no rehabilitation of image or purpose to be offered to her. She knew once they found her alive it was either death by fire or something else. She grabbed the last bottle of bush tea in the cupboard along with the photo of her love above the bedroom cabinet, unlocked the back door which no one knew had existed, and walked barefooted through the muddy track which led out of Kona Village and up to St Catherine Hill.

For her, the idea of flight seemed mythical, never really enough to cure the ailment of unbelonging. It removed you from one flux just to thrust you into another; creating an illusion of difference, and she saw no real contentment in exile, whether forced or self-imposed.

Head heavy with heat and a sunken heart, she moved forward like a snake running through wild thrush, her flowing white dress trailing her footsteps as she drank the bottle of bush tea in gulps, heading for the top of the hill.

On the hill she lay on bare ground, surrounded by her only friends, the trees and their crawling attendants. Using her headtie as a pillow she looked to the sky, eyeing the smoke that loomed from her burning abode just down the hill beyond the greenery, and said to the wind, 'It's me, James, your Gloria. I'm on my way,' drifting off to sleep as ants and birds and insects all common and free, came to bid their companion adieu.

HEAVEN HELP US
David Hamilton

I COULD HEAR everyone's breath as the five of us crammed together waiting Brother Brendan out. My stomach floated high up in my neck and my lungs felt like welding rods in my chest with all the excitement and drama. It was uncomfortable – leaves scratching you, fellas' sweat rubbing on you. I felt like I just smoke a five ball – floating from the potent combination of knocking about boldface when you supposed to be in the people classroom and the very real potential of a swift burial, no crix or coffee, if we get ketch and my parents find out. The movements was plenty but the silence was thick like mud.

It was clear Brother Brendan knew something was off. From where we was set up, you could see the blindingly white robe and his stumpy muscled frame oscillating back and forth. What the principal of a whole prestige school doing patrolling this hour? Even two minutes after second bell he still patrolling; everybody done gone in side and he still watching. Waiting. Just like we.

Out of the crew, I was the only one who place in the top ten in test. Well, top five to be exact. I was still new to this breaking class thing. In my family it was school, home and church, no idling or liming in the street. Homework started 5:30 p.m. sharp, then news, maybe a little time to use the internet then in bed by 9. Church was 8 a.m. sharp every Sunday and the whole family had to come out. I never went any house parties. School bazaars I was home long before the sweaty jam session in the disco started.

I not a nerd eh, but since the age of six, when Mrs Graham tell my father I couldn't see the board properly, I wearing

Island Voices **123**

glasses. My father is a man who all about functionality, he eh have time for finding something cool. Cool? What is that? Value is measured in how long something could last; the sturdier the better. When the dust clear, I end up with the sturdiest grandfather square frames or rather the thickest, Coke bottle, Kareem Abdul-Jabaar welding goggles in the whole shop.

Next thing I know, everybody calling me 'nerd' and despite my best efforts, the name stick. Steve Urkel. Poindexter. You name it. Any nerd you could think of, I get call. It didn't matter that since Form Three I was the only one who could dunk a basketball with ease. Once these glasses on, is disrespect. Just a week ago, Darin, a boy so tiny he could barely reach the blackboard, go look to interfere with me. 'Boy Mark, your glasses so thick you could see the molecular structure of a protein,' Darin said to generous guffaws around the class during Biology.

To that I promptly replied, 'Yes, that's true Darin. I does use it to examine the molecular structure of your mother nanny.'

The whole class imploded unto itself with that one. For minutes after there was a chorus of convulsing screams and heckling. After that, the lecture was done for that period.

That one get me put out of class and the only reason they didn't call my father was because my grades good and I doh really give trouble normally. But I was starting to get fed up with the disrespect.

'Doh poke yuh nose dey boy he go see,' Thomas hissed, and I quickly stepped back before slowly returning to my original position.

'He still there Thomas?' Damian asked.

'Yeah he eh moving,' Thomas answered.

'You think he have the penance with him?' I asked.

Brother Brendan might be a holy brother but he wasn't no priest. When it come to discipline, the quiet sermon coming attached to a swift uppercut to ribs or several devious strokes from a strap that was as thick as a bicycle tyre. We called that strap 'the penance'.

'Boy don't make that joke nah,' said Damian.

Five minutes later and Brother Brendan was still watching. He surveyed the Sixth Form block, across by the wall that fellas would shimmy down and slip out the back gate, down in the big drain next to the stand pipe (another favourite hiding spot) and then cascading upwards across to where we were crammed together, sweaty and hidden behind the overgrown hedge.

'Why he still watching? Like somebody tip he off?' Thomas asked in frustration.

We were all beginning to get antsy.

After one more brisk lap, he surveyed again, one last time. Finally, flicking his long robe behind him he strode towards the tunnel that led to the Form Three block and disappeared into the darkness. Still we waited. Only when the din of misbehaving boys on that side dissipated did we look to make a move. Thomas turned to us with a mischievous look in his light brown eyes – they danced like fireflies beneath his ruffled hair. It was go time.

As a crew we were a band of mercenaries. Damian was my best friend and everybody else's friend too, but the rest ah we wasn't friend. All of us meet through him. He was an enigma in a lot of ways. Slim built, well matchstick really, but fearless. Quiet but more charismatic than the loudest of fellas. Dishevelled but somehow his sloppy was the sloppy girls was interested in. I tried to imitate that level of 'doh care' in dress but neither the girls nor my parents were impressed. It was through Damian I start cutting class.

Maybe the rest of them was a similar story because I sure they didn't like me either. Perms was a little red boy who used to lime with dem white boys and felt he was too good to talk to me.

His specialty was being the right mixture of short and cute that girls wanted to put in their pocket. Thomas was an impish pest with permanently unkept hair and light brown eyes who loved to make bad joke that supposed to be prank. His favourite trick was flicking a lighter by my pants and holding it there until I realised I was on fire. Two of my good school pants had holes because of this idiot. The last fella, I can't remember his real name, but we called him 'Half Pack' because you could not find he without a half pack of Du Maurier cigarette in he pocket. He was a dark Indian with messily slicked back hair and thick glasses, even thicker than mine, so the other popular name for him was 'Mechanic'.

Whatever our differences, we had a common goal. Immediately we assumed our practised routine – single file and brisk but not too fast, with a business-like as if heading to class pace. Even though Brother Brendan was occupied you could never be sure which eyes could appear. The long covered walkway was the tensest part because it was open on both sides – crossing it felt like walking a tightrope. We endured it as long as we could with a practised posture of a slightly bent back and hurried but not hurried crawl and as soon as the area ended we peeled off, slithering by the cold water standpipe and around the unfinished red brick wall. Instead of heading straight under the tunnel as we planned, we took a left up a flight of stairs.

'Wait nah, is the Chapel we going to?' I asked breathlessly as we ascended the first stairwell.

'Yeah wham? You 'fraid God strike you dong?' asked Thomas.

Crouching low, we scampered up the winding stairs until we reached the top.

Damian arrived first and slid the glass door wide open for two of us at a time to skate in. When everyone was inside, I stopped at the door and turned to Damian.

'Whappen Mark? You alright?' he asked.

'Damian look, I feel I going back in class there you know. I just eh really feeling this if I being honest.'

'Chill nah. It going and be a cool scene,' Damian said with a reassuring smile, and for a while I thought I was fine. But as I walked through the chapel door, I looked up and saw a particularly violent Jesus on the crucifix, with thorns above the door frame – the artist actually took the time to paint red areas around the nails that were hammered into his outstretched hands and feet.

'Damian, I doh really ha to be on this one you know. I could just duck back in class quick. I know the route back so Brother Brendan eh go ketch me.'

Damian stopped and considered me for a moment. All the fellas was already inside so it was just us. His face got serious – this was usually his demeanour when it was just the two ah we.

'Mark, I don't really feel good on these limes if you not here. But if you really want to go back I go understand,' he said.

I gave one last look at the school courtyard below – it was completely clean because everyone was in class. But I remembered the last adventure I missed out on and how jealous I felt. That time, they cut class high up on Sando hill and smoked weed and ended up bouncing up a big macajuel in the bush though they eventually found out it was dead long time.

Reluctantly I entered the chapel and with a quick knee bend I made the sign of the cross. I kept my eyes open so I could do it without the fellas noticing.

The Chapel from the outside looked like many other rooms in the school but inside it was like stepping into Narnia. It was a full mini-church complete with multiple rows of polished maple-wood pews on a delicately crafted diagonal-patterned latticed floor below two hanging giant ceiling fans with LED lights that glowed in the dark. Around the church was ample exotic vegetation and beautiful frescoes that was either painted by Michelangelo himself or a really good imitation.

It was the best that alumni money could buy as nothing exuded prestige like praising God expensively. Most important to us, it was the only room in the school with working AC and a giant one at that – the five of us stood in front, hungrily lapping up the cool blasts from the surprisingly silent monstrosity.

Suddenly we heard a voice in front: 'You all are not supposed to be here!'

A person spun authoritatively from the front pew to face us with his arms crossed. It was Gregory.

Gregory was a towering, doughy boy one year ahead of us who most in the school treated with little respect. He was even on a lower rung than me. The easiest of insults was to focus on his teeth which, despite braces, stretched outward like a gymnast hoisting their legs parallel on the balance beam.

Another popular one was to say that he had 'Pamela Anderson tits' and to ask which one was bigger. The cruelest ones would make fun of him for being albino, crafting crude jokes about his racial identity, some even going as far as to call him 'honkey' even though both his parents darker than me. But that chupidness was only tolerated outside the chapel. Up here was his domain.

'I going to have to tell Brother Brendan eh. You all will get me in trouble,' Gregory said. All of us gasped. I looked around the crew and every man looked bummy. Except Damian.

Damian was cool like two block of ice in a mauby glass. He smiled seductively, raking his fingers through his perfectly messy straight hair.

'Was your scene, Gregs? We not causing no trouble. Why you trying to cause trouble?' Damian turned to us winking and clasped both hands with natural comedic timing. 'We just here to say some prayers.' All of us laughed.

'Don't try that. Brother Brendon leave me in charge here—'

'Yes, you in charge, you in charge,' Damian added quickly. 'Come sit with we nah.'

By this time the rest of the fellas had left their school shirts hanging to 'dry' by the AC and were relaxing on the back pew in their under jerseys. I thought about taking off my shirt but decided to keep it on.

Gregory flicked his tongue over his braces and blinked.

'We only here 'til Geography class done. Sit dong nah,' Damian said, pressing the advantage.

Finally Gregory relented. 'That's till 1:45 eh. And mark you all name down in the book,' he said.

We got up and signed the book, the other guys used their usual pseudonyms: 'Broken Penis', 'Load ah toots', 'Weak Viagra', dem kinda thing. They giggled hysterically, jostling each other.

We occupied the two pews at the back left corner of the chapel. Perms lounged in the left corner with his back against the wall and defiantly rested both black Nike Air Maxes on the pews. A blue bandanna with star patterns covered his face and a slim silver chain lay prone and glistened on his spotless white tee. Thomas was slouched in front of him, with one knee on the bench and the other leg on the floor. Gregory was on the same pew as Thomas but contorted his bulbous body so he could stay in the conversation while still sitting 'properly'.

Damian sat opposite Perms. He didn't wear under jerseys so he was in a vest with a gold cross buried in his dark chest hairs. His shoes were also up on the bench – expensive Nike Huaraches but dirty and with no laces, rocking brands just the way I would like to, nonchalantly.

Island Voices

I stood to the side of Damian and leaned against the back of the bench. If I was going to stay here at least my discomfort would be the bargain for my transgressions. Half Pack was by the door as the look out. This was our 'Last Supper' picture. Suddenly, we heard a commotion at the door.

'Who's that now?' Thomas asked.

'Fellas, fellas, this is where you all holding class now.' We turned to see Michael Mendel storming through the sliding door with a villainous grin. As he passed Half Pack at the door, he pelted a hard elbow to his ribs invoking a high pitched yelp. Half Pack doubled over in pain.

Out of all the fellas in the school, Michael was the one you definitely didn't want to go round. It wasn't that he was big or anything. In size he wasn't all that imposing. He wasn't short but he wasn't particularly tall either. He had a somewhat muscular stocky build with large shoulders and veiny forearms, the kind you get from a hard life but there was plenty beefier gym rats in our class alone, far less the school. There was bad boys and brawlers in the school who liked nothing better than a fight and loved to share licks but even those bruisers feared him and showed him copious amounts of respect – to my knowledge Michael Mendel never engaged in any fight. This made us even more fearful.

If I had to point to something I would say it was his face – there was a hardness to his countenance and expression only possible if a boy see things he shouldn't have seen at too young an age. His face looked like several boulders arranged together and decorated with faint scars – it was the style at the time to dice your eyebrows but his wasn't style – it was permanently slashed by something ... or someone.

From the first day Michael walked through those school gates he set a tone one time. In Form One when the boldest ah we was coughing on cigarette smoke he was already trafficking weed to big men in Form Six. However, trafficking was not just a school offence, it was a criminal offence with real repercussions. Half the entire next year we didn't see him – rumour was that police lock he ass up and throw him in Youth Training Camp with other under-age criminals. We wasn't even sure we would ever see he again.

When he returned instead of being more aggressive he seemed slightly reformed, but that was just in demeanour – he wasn't selling ganja no more but graduated to a multitude of problematic albeit less criminal hustles, all of which couldn't really be linked to him.

Michael acquired a police-issue taser gun and started electrocuting students for fun. This action was never actually witnessed but multiple students pants leg stuck to them due to static electricity. When the heat started to raise on that, he became the mastermind behind a ring that stole students' book bags and sold the contents to the second-hand book store on High Street. When that started getting linked to him, he diversified into robbing fundraising events on the school compound. Their most memorable heist was the 'Bess Juice' event that the Boy Scouts was holding to raise money to buy badges. After four of them made off with the giant orange cooler full of cherry Kool-Aid mix and lemon juice, they proceeded to tote it to the other side of the school where they sold it half price at $1 a cup.

Michael's recent hustle was less complicated but possibly his most lucrative one yet. It was a pair of dice. The hustle was simple. He challenged you to a game, a variation on the popular Lucky 7 game that was running like wildfire through many a Church bazaar. You made a bet, either over seven, under seven or seven and then rolled the dice. If you guessed correctly then you got your money back plus a dollar. If you guessed seven correctly you got your money back plus three dollars. The odds weren't favourable and most didn't really want to play, but intimidation made the game popular. Every day Michael went home with no less than $300 in profit.

'Damian!' Michael bellowed, brandishing a wad of cash in his hand. 'I see you have the whole crew here.' He pulled out a square, folded, black bandana out of his back pocket and wiped his dark forehead. After a dramatic pause he smiled and looked around at all of us like he was mentally counting dollars.

'Michael, I not playing no lucky seven with you eh. I done give you $20 for the week already,' Damian said smiling with great effort.

'Don't worry yourself Dames,' said Michael. He slapped Damian on his back and elicited a silent smiling grimace, 'I sure these other fellas want to win some money too. Ent?' he said, turning to me. 'I sure you want to win a little money.

Refusing Michael wasn't a healthy life decision but gambling in the Chapel was real evil thing, at least in my mind. Luckily for me, I didn't have two shillings to rub together – my father didn't believe in allowance.

'I dry boy Michael,' I said with the biggest show of regret I could muster. This was not taken well. As his smile began to demonically fade I quickly added, 'I eh lying. You can check my pockets if you want.' I pulled out both pockets for emphasis, even the back pockets. A thread and a piece of lint lazily descended to the floor. It was comical but nobody laughed.

'Was he name?' Michael asked, not to me, but to Damian.

'Daiz mih boy Mark. He a bright boy too, always in the top five in test,' Damian answered.

'Top five you say?' Michael watched me curiously. 'And you liming with these slackers?' He observed me closely for a while, nodding with a frozen smile. 'You know what,' he said, breaking the silence, 'I go spot you the five dollars. I like your vibes. But you have to play.' He turned to Perms whose foot was no longer on the pew. 'And you too Perms.'

'Michael I eh ha no money either—' started Thomas.

'Hush your mouth,' Michael said, interrupting Thomas with a resounding slap to the back of his shaved head. We jumped at the brutal sound of it and was quickly reminded that skin teeth didn't remove menace. 'You don't come in the top five in test so you cyah fool me. Bring your money out! You too sugar tits,' he said, referring to Gregory who was now wishing he did sell we out from the start. He slapped down the money in the centre of the aisle, smack down on the red carpet that guided the procession from the entrance to the altar. The carpet was filled with saints and the money landed on St Martin's nose. Hypnotically we settled in the pews on either side of him.

'What about Half Pack?' Thomas asked.

'Boy!' Michael said as he sized up to swing another back hand. Thomas cowered, crouching low and making himself small. I feared for him because he covered his head but left his whole back exposed, especially that sensitive area at the small of the back. Michael saw it too and sized up for an epic one but decided against it.

'As I tell you,' he said grabbing his ear, 'you doh come high in test like mih boy here so hush your mouth. If he playing, who go watch the door?' Thomas nodded in acknowledgement with a stupid grin plastered on his face.

'Mechanic! Bring two cigarette dey,' Michael commanded. Half Pack patted his pocket and trotted briskly across before returning to his post.

We played and played. Despite myself I started to enjoy it. Maybe it was the fact that I was winning. Every single round

Island Voices

I won. From the five dollars Michael seeded me I was now up twenty. Thomas was three dollars down. Gregory was up one dollar. Perms was a rich boy so he had to break a hundred note to play – he was down twenty-one dollars. My competitive juices started to flow and I began to forget where I was.

'I putting five on seven, Mikey. I on a hot streak, doh let me get cold in this AC,' I said, waving my wad of money.

'Ah boy! The bright boy figure out the game allyuh. What about you Thomas?' Michael asked.

'Boy Mike, I already dip into my travel money …'

'I eh ask you all that. What you taking?'

Thomas pulled out the seven dollars and looked long at it. I almost felt sorry for him. Is ten dollars he needed to travel home so he was already short. The usual smirk on his face was gone.

'Hurry up we eh have all day,' said Michael growing impatient.

'One dollar on under,' Thomas mumbled.

'Gimme five dollars on over,' Perms said. He watched me hard as he slammed his money on the pile. 'Bright boy cyah win whole day.'

'I go take two dollars on seven too,' said Gregory. He had begun betting what I was betting.

'Ok boys, well is decision time now. Somebody going to win and somebody going to lose,' said Michael. He picked up the pair of dice, kissed them and rocked them two and fro with both hands.

While he was rolling the dice I looked back and realised Damian was staring at me angrily. I was taken aback because we never fall out and I eh know what I do to vex him. As I looked back at him he quickly looked away. This exchange didn't miss Michael.

'Whappen Dames, you find the bright boy winning too much?' he asked facetiously. There was no greater string puller in the school.

When Damian looked at me again he was even more angry. He was one of those you really had to push to get heated but I could see the steam coming off him. He walked straight up to Michael; they was roughly the same height though Michael was a good bit beefier. When he reached him, he stood seething; they was almost nose to nose.

'You cyah leave things alone eh? You always ha to prove a point,' Damian barked through clenched teeth.

Michael laughed sardonically. 'How is my fault he like the game?'

'I getting fed up of you. You always ha to overdo it,' Damian said, pointing in his face.

Michael turned his back to Damian laughing, making a show that the threat was insignificant. When he realised no one else was, he got serious.

'Look boy, get your finger out my face before I break it,' he said as he pelted away the dice. They ricocheted off the giant glass missal stand in front the altar and made an echoing sound. All smile disappeared and his features looked demented – drawn and ghoulish. The real devil had come out.

I was afraid for Damian. I didn't see him coming out of this alive. I wished he would back down but I didn't see it happening either.

'You feel everybody 'fraid you? You feel everybody 'fraid you? Let me show you something.' Damian reached in his pocket and pulled out a large pocket knife. As he flicked it open, Michael shrank back, covering the eye with the scar over the eyebrow.

With all the commotion going on it started to get noisy. I looked to the door and noticed it was wide open with no Half

Pack around. Heavy purposeful footsteps were ascending and everyone get quiet because we all knew who it was and it wasn't Half Pack.

Brother Brendan emerged through the door without making the sign of the cross and barrelled towards us. He scanned the room quickly. On the right was white shirts hanging using his $10,000 AC like a washerwoman's clothesline. In front was a pile of red, green and blue money on the floor like a drunken game of wapee in a hawk and spit bar on the wharf. Smiling to the left was Michael Mendel, the orchestrator, the devil himself in this holy place. Luckily Damian had the presence of mind to slip the knife out of sight.

Brother Brendan made a mad rush towards us. I believe he meant to beat every man like Jesus did in the synagogue, but he stopped himself when he reached me. His thick eyebrows furrowed as he watched Damian, then Michael and then me. His face softened into intense disappointment as our eyes met. It hit me to the core.

'Sir, I tell them not to—' Gregory started.

'Shut up boy!' Brother Brendan barked curtly. Gregory scratched his sandy head and demurely covered his teeth with large, chapped pink lips.

'All of you will meet me in my office immediately,' he said quietly, shaking with anger. 'Now!' he bellowed, exploding before storming out.

All of us head down the stairs in single file without saying a word. The courtyard wasn't clean no more. Everyone was watching.

As we was walking out, like murderers on the way to death row, I asked Damian a flurry of questions, 'What happen there boy? Why you pull that knife on Michael? What trip you off so? I vex you?'

He didn't answer, not even one.

When we almost reached the office Damian looked at me with a look, but it was a look I didn't recognise. It was disappointment.

'From now on make sure and go to class. I eh want to see you cutting class no more.'

REMEMBER ME

Dianne Loton-Franklyn

TIME HEALS ALL wounds, they say, but I have often wished that time would help me to forget. I have learnt that such thoughts are just childish musings of a reality that can never be. For me, time has been a cruel task master lashing without mercy on a back laced with open wounds – wounds raw with wanton memories. The fact that I cannot forget these memories is curious though because I have always had a fairly unremarkable memory. I rarely remember birthdays, anniversaries, names or faces but, to my torment, my recollection of that day remains as fresh as the dew on the hibiscus flowers that she used to pick from her garden – flowers that she used to place in that foggy Coca Cola bottle in the centre of the dining room table anchored by a crisp white starched crochet doily. 'Fresh flowers make me happy,' she used to say. It's funny the memories you remember but far from funny are the memories that you just can't seem to forget.

Even now, I can still recount every minute of that day as if it had been this very moment. It has been almost twenty years and I can still see her face – that gentle face that time can never age and her enviable beauty that was as much on the inside as it was on the outside. She had a small bust, a slender waistline and a real Caribbean posterior which was unusual for a woman with such strong Jewish bloodline, but then my mother was no ordinary woman. She always wore a smile and there wasn't a neighbour in need that she didn't try to help. 'Take this bag over to Ms Cherrie, Deanna and don't give me any attitude, God bless us to bless others.' Memories like that make me smile, but back then I wasn't smiling.

After a long day she used to sit at the dinner table for hours after preparing our evening meal although she always made sure that the dishes were washed and put away almost immediately after we had eaten. After all 'no well thinking woman' would leave dirty dishes in the sink for extended periods or worse, overnight. I sighed – to this day I still wash the dishes almost immediately after I have eaten.

Her 'office' was red, white and shiny; she loved that Formica and chrome Dinette set. She was so proud when she bought it. She had saved for months and we were all so excited when it was delivered to our gate. All the neighbours came out to see it and she was proud to let them have a peek. From the moment it arrived it was as if she designated it as her own private retreat – where she could think and feel and dream of who she might have been.

She always ended the day there and I always watched her from my kneeling perch on the sofa. In those moments when she seemed to drift away, I wished that I could read her mind – I always wanted to know 'her' – the woman before she knew my father, before she had kids.

She was a simple woman and we lived a simple life, but even at the age of ten I knew that she had imagined her life differently, though she would never admit it. 'Stop staring, Deanna,' she would say with a smile, 'go get ready for bed.' Her voice was always gentle and kind; I don't think that I ever heard her raise her voice, at least not before that day, but then there are many things that I never knew about her before that day.

The Sunday before that day began like any other with a tickle on the sole of our feet and my daily disgust at mom's method of awakening us. She never ever paid attention to our protests though, she would only say, 'It's time to get up, the birds have been up for hours now.' To this I would reply, 'I wish you were mother to those birds instead of me' (although I must confess that this response was always from the safety of my mind).

She was especially chirpy that day as she prepped the red peas for the rice and peas – a Sunday dinner staple. I can still smell the freshly cut thyme and green onions, the unforgettable aroma of Scotch bonnet pepper simmering in freshly prepared coconut milk and her signature ingredient – lots of garlic – and a piece of salted beef. In the background Dad played Jim Reeves while we unwillingly completed our chores.

My dad was a quiet man but I never understood him. I could not reconcile how such a seemingly loving dad (at least to my sisters) could be so controlling. I hated the control he exerted over my mother, and I hated when he shouted at her – and always for the same thing:

'Petrona, how hard is it to remember to take your vitamins and why won't you let me know when you are leaving the house.'

I always wondered about that. I mean, who nags their wife about taking vitamins and who always needs to know the whereabouts of their wife at every given moment? I'll tell you who – a controlling cheating bastard, at least that was how my friend Terry put it. She said her dad was the same way and it turned out that he was cheating with Miss Ivy just one street over on Newberry Drive, which is why he always wanted to know where her mom was.

My dad never seemed like the cheating type, although it would have explained a lot if he was. I was never close to him because I could never break though his prison guard exterior. The same tone with which he spoke to the prisoners was the same tone in which he spoke to us (Mom and me) and although he was mostly gentle with my sisters I was never really sure if he was capable of loving anyone, least of all my mother.

She had met him when she was only 16 years old. He was ten years her senior and her parents never approved of him. She came from an affluent family in the equally affluent community of Belvedere Heights and, to make matters worse, he was dark skinned and she could have easily passed for a Caucasian beauty on any given day of the week. Her parents never approved of dark-skinned suitors, whether they were wealthy or not. She had told us that her mother would say that anything that was black was only suited for the trash. This was the only glimpse that we ever got of our maternal grandparents. We never met them and they were rarely made mention of in our house.

She had met Dad when he visited her house to sell life insurance. She told us that she had loved him instantly and in the end she ran away with him to Kingston when she was only 17 years old. She had tried to reconcile with her parents but they could never forgive her. Once she told me that she had wanted to be a school teacher and teach at The Immaculate High, but those dreams were long gone.

Belvedere too was a distant dream. The clustered concrete low-income housing community of Northsand was now her reality. Before 'that day', she had been a room attendant for 14 years at the Roston Rose Hotel. She worked long days but I never heard her complain. She still cooked us dinner every evening and tucked us in at nights. She raised her girls to be proud of who they were and she never played favourites. I loved that about her.

Dad on the other hand was a good provider but I often wondered if he had the same ideology as my maternal grandparents. In our family, I was 'the dark one' and my sisters were 'the brown ones' and to make matters worse, they had long curly hair. The combination was a definite plus in our community and in society on the whole. They were loved and admired and to Dad they could do no wrong. Aside from being dark skinned, my hair was a tangled mess that used to break every comb until Mom bought an iron comb – that fixed that problem, but my scalp was forever sore.

I remember Dad stroking my sisters' hair and telling them that he loved them. His hands never stroked my hair and I never heard those words, not once. At those times I could see a gentler man, even if his tenderness was not towards me. He never treated me badly but he never showered me with affection either. I often thought of running away but I could never leave my mom; it would break her heart and I could never do that to her. I loved her too much and I knew she loved me with the same ferocity, but I was a child and children don't always understand everything.

Dinner that Sunday consisted of fried chicken, rice and beans, macaroni salad and carrot juice sweetened with tinned milk. Dad had commented that she had outdone herself. We all took a bath and watched the Sunday matinee as we always did, then we chatted and ironed our uniforms for school. That night I remember her kissing me on the forehead and saying as she always did, 'Love you always D' and I mumbled, 'Love you Mums.'

I woke up to sobbing and yelling. I stumbled out of my room to find my mom curled up on the ground in the corner of the living room. She was sobbing and my dad yelling that he couldn't take it anymore. He rushed towards her and I instinctively leaped to protect her but he just kneeled down beside her and begged her to think of our family. I didn't know what that meant but I remembered my sisters crying and hanging on to me. My dad sent us to get ready for school and we left the living room confused and dazed.

That morning we said goodbye to our mom from her private space at the dinner table. Her smile was sad that morning. If only I had kissed her goodbye and said, 'Love you Mom.' Maybe she would have reconsidered, but that is water under the bridge as my mother used to say.

Before that day I don't believe that I had ever seen her look sad. Dad was quiet that morning as we walked to the bus stop and he barely told us goodbye when he exited the bus at his stop. My sisters asked about what had happened that morning as we walked to school, but all I could do was hug them and count down the hours until I could get back home to see her.

My sisters and I got home at 4.00 p.m. The lock on the gate was open and the front door was ajar. This was not unusual but there was no smell of curried chicken (with strong note of garlic) and boiled bananas, which was the menu for Mondays and the house seemed quiet. 'Moms,' I called. 'Mommy,' my sisters cried out. 'Maybe she went to the shop?' I said, but I knew she hadn't gone to the shop. She would never have left the door open. Something was wrong, I could feel it.

I sent my sisters to change their clothes and as I looked around the house hoping to find her I saw a note scribbled on the refrigerator. It simply said, 'Remember me'. It was her handwriting but what did it mean? 'Remember me' – that phrase haunts me. I stared at that note for what seemed like hours. Where was she? Would she come back? That evening as I fixed corned beef sandwiches for my sisters, my head spun and I felt nauseous. This must have been how Jenna felt when her dad went away,-but this was different. I knew that she would be back.

I remember showing Dad the note that evening and he just froze. I rushed home every day that week expecting to smell the distinctive note of garlic coming from the kitchen, but I only found silence – worse than silence, I didn't find Moms.

Island Voices

That kind of betrayal shatters you in a way that you can never explain. My sisters were only five and six years old respectively but they were no less affected. The most shocking of all though was my father. He walked around for months like a shadow. He was crushed. Somehow I thought he would have been relieved but he wasn't. He searched for her for months and he made reports at what seemed like every police station and he even went to see her parents. It was as if she never existed. She had vanished. Our house was never the same again, we would never again see her smile, we would never hear her hum, 'What a Friend we have in Jesus,' and we would never hear 'Love you always' ever again (at least not from her). All we had left were memories, a note and many unanswered questions.

On the day that I graduated from university all I wanted to do was to see my mom, but the only parent I had left was my dad so I went to see him. He never came to see me collect my teaching degree, only my sisters and my fiancé came. That day that marked so much accomplishment for me felt especially sad and so I left everyone to go see my dad. Sitting in the living room on his favourite chair with his feet up on the hassock staring at her Dinette set he seemed different. He seemed broken. As I entered through the door he looked up at me and for the first time I could see genuine affection.

'I love you, Deanna. I have never told you that before, but I love you and I am so proud of you. I always knew that your mother would leave and I resented you for being so much like her. Sit down.' he said.

I just slumped down on the sofa in disbelief ... did I hear him correctly? Was he dying? Or was he planning on leaving too?

'I don't expect you to forgive me but I need you to know the truth. The first year your mother and I were married I came home one evening to find you crying in your crib and your mother gone. I searched for her everywhere and she didn't return for four days. When she returned she looked like she had been living on the street and that is when she told me that she had been diagnosed with schizophrenia when she was 14 years old. She told me that her mother and grandmother had both suffered from the disease. I didn't know what to say,' he continued 'but I knew that I loved her.'

He further explained that the vitamins that he had pressed her over the years to take was really her medication. He told me that the doctor's had said that I might have inherited my mother's illness.

'It was stupid, Deanna, but I thought that if I got close to you it would have been that much more difficult to accept losing you to that terrible illness. I know now that I was wrong. The day that your mother went away, we were arguing because she told me that she hadn't taken her medication for over two weeks. I begged her to take them but she said she felt lost and empty when she took them and that she didn't want to feel that way anymore. She thought that she could control it but, she couldn't. You mustn't blame your mother, Deanna, a mother has never loved her family more, but the truth is that she could not control her thoughts and actions when she was off her medication.'

As I drove home I could not contain my tears. Was my mother living on the streets or was she dead? Could I or my sisters develop schizophrenia? What if I have a child who has it? A part of me wished that my mom was dead because to me the alternative was worse. Now every time a pass a homeless person I look to see if it's HER – my moms – but sometimes admittedly with shame. I also wish that I never see her again so that I can remember her as she was.

Since then, my relationship with my father has been much improved. We still have mending to do but I have no doubt that we will get there. These days when I talk to him on the phone I end by saying, 'Love you always, Dad' and he says it right back.

On this my wedding day my emotions are bitter sweet; as my father walks me down the aisle I can't help but remember the note that my mother left on the refrigerator.

As I prepare to leave for my honeymoon I remove her picture from its secret place in my wallet. Her face remains the same and her smile is happy, she sits on 'her office chair', so calm and stately, her face beaming. I let my tears flow freely and as I kiss her face I whisper, 'I'll always remember you, Moms, love you always.'

CREATURES IN THE ACKEE TREE

Kathleen A Chaitoo

From I born til now, my granny always used to tell me, child, never you pick and eat ackee at night. I used to always beg her to tell me why but, the ol' foot always put up a fight. Is when I grow big and hard time lick me, I fully understand why granny always preach. Child, ackee at night, never you pick and eat.

***

IT WAS TWO days before Christmas and I was seventeen years old. It was the year that I dropped out of school, as I could not afford it anymore. I had recently gotten a job up at the old sugar factory and was coming home from work one evening. That day, as I recall, was one of the most miserable days of my life.

After waiting almost a month, Mas Peter told me that I still would not be able to get paid until after the holiday. I was feeling so hopeless, wondering where I was going to get the next cent from. Plus, to top it all off, I had been running on an empty stomach since yesterday.

When I got home I searched my kitchen from top to bottom, in hopes of finding any food at all. But, there was not a crumb in sight. I checked all over the house for loose change. From every pocket in every pair of pants that I owned to the crevices of the settee. I searched every crack, corner and pinhole. After looking tirelessly and still coming up with nothing, I got so frustrated that I decided to just go and sit out in the backyard.

As I stepped out into the night air, the first thing that caught my eyes was a beautiful bunch of ackee pods hanging on a low limb. I started fantasising immediately. I imagined the plate of barefoot ackee right in front of me. The freshly chopped tomatoes, onions, scallions, garlic and not to mention the tantalising scotch bonnet pepper that I could already taste in my mouth.

I wasted not a moment more. I fetched my hook stick and picked every single ackee I could find. I quickly shelled and cleaned them, then put them on to boil. In the meantime, I went to pick the ingredients from my neighbour's garden. After I got them, I returned to the kitchen and made the most mouth-watering plate of ackee I had ever eaten in my entire life. I went to bed that night with a smile on my face. Though my pockets were empty, my belly was full and I could not have been happier. The day might have been terrible but I had hope that tomorrow would be better.

Later on that night, in the early hours of the morning, I started dreaming some strange things. I was in the kitchen and a ginormous rat, about the same size as me, was sitting around my dining table. I let out a deafening scream and took up the frying pan to kill it. As I was about to strike it, the strangest thing happened.

'Trevor, you nyam di ackee?!' it asked.

'Granny?! A you that?' I shouted.

Then all of a sudden my belly started to glow. I started to panic.

'Yes man, see it deh,' she uttered.

'Granny, what happening to me?' I pleaded.

She started laughing hysterically.

'Granny?!'

'Ha-ah-ha-ah-ha-ah-ha,' she continued to cackle.

I jumped out of my sleep immediately; my heart was going a mile a minute. Then, I saw something incredibly unusual. The veins in my arm seemed as though they were glowing! I rubbed my eyes, as I thought I must still be dreaming. I decided to pay no mind to it, simply to ignore it and go back to bed. Obviously, I was still asleep. Yes, I was still dreaming.

Morning came and I woke to the beautiful rays of the sun, shining through my window. I hopped out of bed and went to open it. The birds were chirping in perfect harmony, the morning dew smelled delightful and there was a gentle wind in the air. It was a glorious morning. I took a deep breath of that fresh morning air and stretched as far as my arms allowed me. I then went into the bathroom to get ready for the day. I stood in front of the sink, got my toothbrush, then as soon as my eyes glanced at the mirror, I saw it.

'No, no, no, no. This can't be real. No!' I shouted hysterically.

Somehow, my right eyebrow and the left half of my moustache had been completely shaved off.

I started having a meltdown, right there in the bathroom.

'Why lord?! Why me?!'

'Why do bad things happen to beautiful people?', I uttered dramatically.

As I sat there sobbing, the dream I had last night suddenly came back to my memory. I recalled my grandmother asking, 'Trevor, you nyam di ackee?'

I wondered if this might have had anything to do with these events. I shrugged it off. I thought, there was absolutely no way eating some ackee at night could have caused this. I got up and went to the kitchen, making sure to avoid all mirrors. As I entered my kitchen, what happened next no one would believe. Chickens! Red hens perched all over my kitchen and they weren't normal chickens, no. They were dressed in Christmas decorations: garlands, ornaments, lights, bells, one even had an angel on its head. Upon closer inspection, I realised that these were all my Christmas decorations.

I stepped backward out of the kitchen slowly and said to myself, 'I need to go see Granny.'

As I was getting ready to go out, one chicken in particular started following me around. As I was brushing my hair, she flew up and sat on my dresser.

'Shew, get away!' I shouted.

It just sat looking at me and nothing I did made it leave. It sat there and watched me until I was finished. As I was about to leave, my stomach started to quiver. I fell against the wall, holding my stomach. Then suddenly out of nowhere, 'Baawk, baawk, bawk, bawk, bawk.' I started making sounds like a chicken and behaving like one.

I clucked all the way to the front door. It wasn't until the chicken started pecking my toes that I was able to snap out of this trance. I was beyond baffled. I did not have the slightest idea of what had happened. I only saw myself in the mirror, posing like a chicken. I put on my hat, sunglasses and a mask in hopes of hiding my face, then left the house immediately. The chicken followed me still.

As I was about to cross the street, I stepped out into the open, and then all of a sudden I went numb. I couldn't move an inch. I tried dragging my feet but it was impossible. Every bit of me was paralysed. I started to tremble, trying my hardest to move my body. However, the only thing that I could move was my eyes.

As I stood there motionless, my ears became flooded by the alarming screams of a man at the top of the road.

'Watch it! Watch it! Di peanut cart get weh!' he shouted.

I fixed my eyes to the furthest corner of my head to see what was going on. I turned them, only to realise that I was about to be struck by this peanut cart that was coming towards me at lightning speed. I started sweating profusely, trying with every bone in my body to move out of the way. I tried and tried but my efforts were useless. I was still unable to move. I closed my eyes and said a prayer, believing strongly that this was going to be the end.

Now, I was not a strong and muscular man. I was skinny, small and unusual. If the wind blew too hard, I would be swept away. I was seventeen years old but, in terms of my body, I looked as if I was seven. So, you can imagine why I was so deathly afraid of this speeding peanut cart. Whereas an average-sized person would receive a few injuries, for me, I would surely be eating peanuts in the sky.

As it was about to hit me, the same mad chicken flew up into my face and broke the trance. She made quite the commotion, so loud in fact that it echoed throughout the neighbourhood. By this, I was now able to move and jumped out of the way, back onto the sidewalk. The cart sped past me, with its owner not too far behind, chasing after it.

I laid on the ground with the chicken on my chest. It was at that moment that I decided to keep her. I named her Nutmeg, the chicken who saved my life. I took her up and continued my journey. As I reached the end of the street, I heard someone crying hysterically. 'Oh god! What am I going to do now? All a me chickens gone!' she shouted, as she continued to cry.

I quickly took up Nutmeg and hid her in my shirt, whispering to her, 'I'll bring you back later,' as I made a quick escape. I was flat out broke, not a cent to my name, so rather than take the bus, I had to walk all the way to Granny's house. This was going to be a treacherous journey, as she lived far away, and reaching her was not going to be an easy feat. Furthermore, my special little problem was going to make it even more difficult.

Island Voices

I conjured up frightening thoughts of what could go wrong: What if I freeze in the middle of a road again? What if I cluck my way into crocodile-infested waters? What if I pick something poisonous and eat it? Or worse, what if I get married to a chicken?! Oh, God.

Nevertheless, I put my fears aside and carried on with my journey. I would have to go past Hill Run, through the orange walk, then stay on the main road and then cross the footbridge up at Blackwell. All this before I would be able to reach Granny.

With my fowl in hand, I began to walk. As I came upon the entrance of Hill Run, the smell of fried chicken lingered in the air. It smelled delightful but then I remembered that I had Nutmeg. If I wasn't careful she could escape and end up in somebody's frying pan! So, I hastily made my way out of Hill Run. As I was almost at the exit, a nasty and devious thought crept into my mind:

'Di chicken smells good. Ask them to fry Nutmeg nuh.'

'No, I can't do that.' I battled with myself.

'Just tell dem seh you have no money but you have a chicken. Them will do it.'

I paid no mind to the thoughts and continued walking. Then all of a sudden my legs swerved, taking me into one of the cookshops.

'Serve! Serve!' I shouted.

'Yes sir?' The cashier asked.

'I don't have any money but I have a chicken, can you fry it fi me?' I asked, with no remorse. She raised her eyebrows and looked at me most strangely.

'Let me ask Mr T,' she said.

She left and went around to the back. A few moments later this very large man came out to greet me. He was as wide as he was tall, and he held a meat cleaver in his hand. His face looked mean and he stared at me as if he wanted to chop *me* up with the cleaver. Suddenly, I came to my senses and decided it was time to leave. As I was about to leave, I heard a soft voice reach out to me.

'You can keep your chicken, there's plenty of food in the kitchen,' he uttered.

I have no idea what came over me next, but as soon as I heard his voice a boisterous and humiliating laugh burst forth. I tried to stop myself but it was as if someone had been controlling me. Then I did something even more unbelievable. I reached over and took up the ketchup and hot sauce bottles and emptied them on his head. I then proceeded to use Nutmeg to slather it all over him, while still laughing. I laughed until I was out of breath. Finally, he had enough and threw me and Nutmeg out of the shop.

As we landed on the ground, I tried to apologise. 'Sir, I am so sorry. Please forgive me,' I begged. Not convinced, he slammed the door in our faces.

Fed up with myself, I got up and went off with Nutmeg.

'Somebody ago kill me today, I just know it,' I said in desperation to the bird.

As we continued to walk, I began attacking strangers with ridiculous phrases. No one was safe, for every person I passed, something insane slipped from my mouth. Things like, 'All hail the frog queen!' and 'I am a carrot.' I had no idea what was happening; the uncontrollable gibberish that was flowing from my mouth could not be stopped. I even told an old lady that one night, the ants were going to come for her so she can be their lawyer. I knew for sure that I would never be able to show my face in that community again.

Thankfully, I was now only a short distance away from the orange walk. As I drew closer, the scent of those citrus wonders greeted me. Then all of sudden I started to feel sick again.

'No, not again,' I worried.

As I entered the orange walk, I felt as if I was going to throw up. Out of nowhere, my feet began to drag, trying to slow me down. I kept pushing, deciding that I was not going to let this stop me again. My hands grabbed onto the fence. Unable to let go, I pulled with all my might and was able to release myself. As I was about to reach the very first tree, my head started to swell, the pain hit me left, right, and centre. I fell to the ground, now having to crawl.

I crawled and crawled. My head felt as if it was about to explode. I fought hard and crawled towards the tree. I got to the tree and as I laid my hand on it, suddenly all my troubles dispersed. I hugged the tree, wrapping my arms and legs around it. I felt free.

'Whatever is inside me, clearly nuh like orange,' I said to myself.

As I sat for a while, petting Nutmeg, a brilliant idea struck me. I would take as many oranges as I could manage and tie them around me. I would use the branches as a walking stick and I'd put the leaves in my pockets. This, I believed, would surely ward off what was inside me. I gathered all the pieces and strung myself up like a Christmas tree.

So said, so done. The oranges worked and I felt normal again. Nutmeg and I continued on our journey. We left the orange walk without a single block in the road. Feeling extremely happy, I picked up Nutmeg and ran like a cheetah along the main road. Finally, I got to Blackwell and I was feeling so relieved that nothing strange had happened.

As I ventured up to the footbridge, I was ready to go across with absolutely no fear. This bridge was just a few pieces of wood, held together by some rope and a couple of nails. It sat above a gently flowing river but, with the recent heavy rains, the river rose. The current also was now much stronger. As I took my first step, the bridge swung sideways. It felt very unsteady. I slowly crept, taking each step as carefully as I could.

I made my way to the middle of the bridge and the next step I took was onto a piece of rotted wood. My foot fell through first and my entire body followed after. I fell into the river and all my embellishments washed away. Not even a single leaf was left.

I got out of the water with Nutmeg perched on my head. 'What am I going to do now?' I wondered.

I did the only manly thing I could think of.

'Grannay! Granny! Mama!' I screamed and ran as fast as I could towards my grandmother's house, which was just around the corner. Before I was able to reach her, I had to creep along the hillside and believe me, it was a long way down. I always hated walking there.

With the chicken on my head, I held onto the rocks, slowly making my way around. I was almost there now, just a few more steps. As I was about to reach the end, I did the most unbelievable thing – I threw myself off the path, diving toward the precipice. Had it not been for a tree branch that had stretched itself out, I would have died. I grabbed it and tried to pull myself up. Just as I was about to reach it, snap! The branch broke and I started to scream. I thought for sure I was dead, so I shut my eyes tight. After screaming and screaming, I heard a voice say, 'Trevor, stop scream, yah frighten the chicken.' The voice was that of my grandmother, who had hooked my collar with her walking stick and had stopped me from falling.

She pulled me up and gave me a suffocating hug.

'How you know seh me did deh here Mama?' I asked.

'Me dream see you last night me chile, come mek we go in,' she replied.

Mama's house was nothing extravagant, a small board house with some trees at the back and a few animals running around. However, the fresh coat of red and white paint that she bought for Christmas, truly brightened it up. The house was simple but my grandmother was no easy woman. She was a typical Jamaican elder, deeply rooted in tradition, and stood by it no matter what.

My grandma was the sweetest woman I had ever known. She would always hug me like she was trying to kill me but that was just her way of showing love. She was a fantastic cook too. Whenever I would be feeling down, she would fry banana fritters or make sweet potato pudding for me, as she knew these were my absolute favourite treats. I loved my mama but, I was terrified at how she would react when I told her what I had done.

As we entered the house, I could not hold it back, the first thing I blurted out was, 'Granny me eat di ackee. Me couldn't help it. Me did affi run a boat inna di night.'

'Me know,' she replied, with a smug look on her face.

'But, how you fi know?' I questioned.

'Me been around longer than you think bwoy.'

'Now, stop di talking an listen,' and she covered my mouth.

'Up in di ackee tree at night,

Live some creatures far from plain sight.

In each pod di likkle crawsis dem dwell,

Ready and waiting, fi mek you head swell.

Foolish people who tink dem know it all,

Eat di ackee at night and stumble and fall.

Pinchy Pego dem name and at night dem come,

Fi sleep inna di ackee, til di mawnin sun.

Nuh be stupid, tek me advice.

Gah you bed hungry. You will be aright ...'

'Why you neva guh turn poet, Mama?' I said to her sarcastically.

'Shut up,' she shouted, as she hit me in the head with her stick.

'Ouch! a joke, a joke! Suh weh me ago do bout them, Mama?' I asked as I rubbed my head.

'Tek a bottle of white rum. Mek a trail from the ackee tree to you head. Pinchy pego love rum, dem will smell it and find dem way home.'

'How you know seh dem like rum?'

'Watch ya, who nuh like rum pickney?'

She then took up Nutmeg and started petting her.

'You know dis same ting did happen to you Uncle. Look like it run inna di family, cause him find a nice chicken too. Dem married and live a country now. He-heh-ya,' she laughed, hysterically.

I fainted immediately. When I woke up it was nightfall. Grandma had put me in her bed to sleep.

A few moments later, my grandma walked in with a big bottle of white rum. As she moved closer to me, my entire body began to glow yellow, and once again the gibberish started to flow. 'Sky juice, calabash, breadfruit, leaves! These are di tings we need fi to be free!' I ranted.

Mama started drenching me in rum, washing me with it from top to bottom. As she did this she started to chant,

'Pinchy pego come and go,

From di body, head to toe,

Leave dis boy an let him be,

Pinchy pego, return to di ackee tree.'

Suddenly, I started saying 'Rum! Rum! Rum how we love it so! Rum! Rum! Rum! Yes, we a come!'

My grandmother continued to chant. She poured a little bit of the rum into my mouth and suddenly my body felt as if it was about to explode. I started to shake and suddenly the yellow glowing moved from all over my body to the centre of my stomach. The light was so bright it lit up the entire room. Then like lava from a volcano, the glowing lights shot up through my mouth! It was mesmerising! These creatures, whatever they were, glowed brighter than the sun.

As they left my body, they stayed suspended in the air. They twinkled in the room, like stars in the night sky. For the first time in my life, I had been able to witness something out of this world. Momentarily they started to flutter, then my grandma poured the rum on the floor.

She made the trail, from the bedroom to the ackee tree out back and they followed it like ants to sugar. When they arrived at the tree, they all spread out, each taking their individual place. The tree glowed in bright lights of yellow.

As we stood there I was amazed at how many of these creatures had invaded my body. No wonder I acted the way I did!

Then Grandma turned to me and said, 'You know son, a usually just one or two Pinchy Pego live in a ackee tree.' I was shocked, but a smile grew upon my face as I thought that I must have truly been special to be chosen by so many.

Then Granny said, 'Weh yah grin for? A Christmas, dem probably just come dung fi the holiday! Wo-hoii!'

MEET THE AUTHORS

Otancia Noel is from Trinidad and Tobago. She has a degree in Mass Communication and Literature from College of Science Technology and Applied Arts of Trinidad and Tobago (COSTAATT) and an MFA in Creative Writing Prose Fiction from the University of West Indies Trinidad. She was longlisted for both fiction and non-fiction writing for the Johnson and Amoy Achong Caribbean Writers Prize. Otancia was the 2021 recipient of the Vincent Cooper Literary Prize and has previously had short stories published in magazines. She teaches and loves reading, writing, cooking and gardening, and is currently working on her first novel from which her short stories were derived.

Fabian D Smith is a Jamaican writer. He started out ghost writing short films and Mangas and has worked as a freelance journalist with the *Jamaica Observer*. He is determined to share a side of Caribbean culture not yet experienced by the world.

Nardia J Grant is from and lives in Jamaica. She holds a Bachelor of Arts Degree in Media and Communication, a Postgraduate Diploma in Language Education and a Master of Education in Educational Planning and Policy. Nardia's working life has been spent in the Jamaican Public Sector in Government Communications. She loves nature and the natural environment as well as languages and has a deep appreciation for other cultures, especially African cultures. She enjoys running and participates in several 5K charity road races in Jamaica each year. Nardia hopes to become a published author and novelist in the future.

Sherena Christmas is from the Commonwealth of Dominica, the Nature Isle of the Caribbean. She attended the University of the West Indies Cave Hill Campus in Barbados and holds a Bachelor of Science degree in Biochemistry with First Class Honours. Sherena is passionate about education and served as a teacher at her alma mater, an all-girls high school in Dominica, for six years. She is currently working towards a career as a clinical scientist, pursuing a Master of Science degree in Biology at the College of William and Mary in Virginia, USA. Sherena has taken part in essay, poetry and short-story competitions since childhood. Most recently, she was the winner of the Short Story Contest of the Dominica Independence Literary Competition 2021. In her leisure time, Sherena enjoys reading, creative writing, music and being in nature.

Rosetta Thomas is a Senior IT Professional from Kingston, Jamaica. She holds a Bachelor of Arts degree in Spanish and Computer Science (Double Major with Honours) as well as a Master of Science Degree in Computing and Information Technology (Distinction). She works in one of Jamaica's leading financial institutions where she leads a team of Application Developers. She has always had a passion for writing and aspires to publish a novel that will highlight the rich heritage of life in rural Jamaica. She is a member of Toastmasters International where she has achieved several public speaking designations and has held several leadership roles over the years.

Sharnna Archat Edmondson is a teacher of English and Information Literacy and has taught for over twenty years at secondary level as well as training adults in Use of English, Customer Service and Digital Literacy. She was also a CXC Assistant Examiner for over five years, specialising in story and summary writing. She holds a Master of Library and

Information Studies degree with distinction and a Bachelor in Education, majoring in English/Literature from the University of the West Indies, together with a Diploma in Education from Mico University in English/Library. Currently, Sharna is a Media Coordinator in North Carolina. She aspires to publish a children's story book as well as short stories based on her experiences growing-up and culture.

Jodianna R Clarke describes herself as an extrovert with introverted tendencies. To say Jodianna has a love for books would be an understatement! In her teenage years, reading *For My Mother (May I Inherit Half Her Strength)* by Lorna Goodison changed Jodianna and gave her a glimpse of the power of writing from our unique experiences. Jodianna has an MSc in Human Resource Development from the University of the West Indies. Professionally she has worked in business process outsourcing, hospitality, health and finance industries, both in communications and in human resources.

Geon Codd is proud to be a homegrown Belizean. Currently possessing an Associate's Degree in English, he plans to pursue further education in corporate law in the near future. Writing has always been his passion, and he continues to take steps to finetune this and hopes to become a published author in the fantasy genre.

Stephanie Ramlogan is a Caribbean writer whose fiction is built around the people, culture and folklore of Trinidad and Tobago. She is the 2022 Iowa Review Fiction Award recipient, and the 2020 Brooklyn Caribbean Literary Festival Elizabeth Nunez Award Caribbean-American writer's prize winner. Stephanie has a Master of Fine Arts in Creative Writing from Brooklyn College in New York City. She is currently revising her first novel.

Claudia Allen-Williams is from St. Catherine, Jamaica, but now lives in Virginia, USA with her family. She holds a Bachelor's degree in English from Texas A&M University and a Masters in Curriculum and Instruction in Gifted Education from George Mason University, Virginia. Claudia is a 30-year veteran educator who presently works in the Fairfax County Public School System where she teaches eighth grade English. This is her first publication.

Akhim Alexis lives in Trinidad and Tobago. He is a PhD student in Literature and Creative Writing at the University of Southern California (USC) and the winner of the Brooklyn Caribbean Literary Festival Elizabeth Nunez Award for Writers in the Caribbean. He was also a finalist for the Barry Hannah Prize in Fiction, Aesthetica Creative Writing Award, the Grist Imagine 2200: Climate Fiction for Future Ancestors Contest, and the Johnson and Amoy Achong Caribbean Writers Prize for Poetry. His work has appeared or is forthcoming in *The Massachusetts Review*, *Obsidian: Literature & Arts in the African Diaspora*, *Electric Literature*, *The Rumpus* and elsewhere.

David Hamilton lives in Trinidad. He holds a Bachelor's degree in Computer Science & Management. His love of writing began with trying to recreate his favourite *Hardy Boys* novels in primary school and progressed to writing scripts for plays, penning passionate music blog posts and crafting the lyrics for his own hip hop song releases under the moniker 'Da Face'. David is the first-place winner of the inaugural Caribbean Magazine Plus Short Story Competition 2022. He is currently working on his debut novel.

Dianne Loton-Franklyn lives on the island of Jamaica. She holds a Bachelor of Science Degree in Psychology and a Masters in Educational Leadership. She has always been interested in Caribbean stories and culture but she also has a deep love for expressing stories about children with special needs who otherwise would not have a voice. She currently works as a behaviour therapist for children and adults with intellectual disabilities.

Kathleen A Chaitoo's interests include writing, art, music and film. She believes there's always a story to be told! Coming from Old Harbour, Jamaica, Kathleen aims to write stories that speak to the hearts of those who read them. She pours love into her writing in the hope that it will show and readers will feel it too.

Also available in the Caribbean Contemporary Classics series:

A Brighter Sun **by Sam Selvon 9781398307759**
Early married life throws up challenges for a young couple in 1940s' Trinidad.

Aunt Jen **by Paulette Ramsay 9781398307742**
Letters from a young girl in Jamaica to her mother in 1970s' Britain.

Bad Girls in School **by Gwyneth Harold 9781398340541**
Three Jamaican teenagers have a chance to turn their lives around.

Beka Lamb **by Zee Edgell 9781398340473**
A coming of age for Beka, against the backdrop of change in Belize.

Cricket in the Road **by Michael Anthony 9781398340497**
Short stories, atmospheric, poignant and entertaining, from the master of Caribbean story telling.

Escape to Last Man Peak **by Jean D'Costa 9781398307766**
An intrepid band of orphans trek across the mountainous terrain of Jamaica to reach a safe haven in the midst of a pandemic.

Green Days by the River **by Michael Anthony 9781398307773**
A coming-of-age story with a difference from one of the master chroniclers of Trinidad.

Letters Home **by Paulette Ramsay 9781398307797**
A Jamaican woman in 1960s' Britain tries to make sense of her experience in the context of her family back home.

Nevile and the Lost Bridge **by Debbie Jacob 9781398307803**
A sci-fi fantasy set in the Caribbean of 2222 from one of Trinidad's most respected authors.

Nevile and the Duppy Master **by Debbie Jacob 9781398340565**
Further adventures of Nevile and friends in part two of this exciting dystopian series.

Old Story Time **by Trevor Rhone 9781398307810**
An inspiring play exploring the insidious effects of racism and corruption, and how individuals can overcome them.

Over Our Way **ed Jean D'Costa and Velma Pollard 9781398307827**
A riotous, poignant, entertaining selection of short stories by top Caribbean authors.

Songs of Silence **by Curdella Forbes 9781398340503**
A luminous, evocative account of vibrant and characterful childhood in rural Jamaica. A magical song of a book.

Sprat Morrison by Jean D'Costa 9781398340527
A fun-filled, action-packed year in the life of Jamaica's favourite schoolboy.

The Sun's Eye ed Anne Walmsley 9781398307841
A wide-ranging collection reflecting the myriad and vibrant life of the Caribbean.

The Wine of Astonishment by Earl Lovelace 9781398340480
Community upheaval, religious conflict and political change in newly independent Trinidad.

The Year in San Fernando by Michael Anthony 9781398340466
Francis' first experience of city life and the complex relationships of adulthood.

The Young Warriors by V. S. Reid 9781398307858
An adventure story set in the free Maroon community in Jamaica during the height of slavery: four young warriors are tested to the limit.

CARIBBEAN CONTEMPORARY CLASSICS

Enduring works of fiction from the heart of the Caribbean

Aunt Jen
A Brighter Sun
Bad Girls in School
Beka Lamb
Cricket in the Road
Escape to Last Man Peak
Green Days by the River
Letters Home
Nevile and the Duppy Master

Nevile and the Lost Bridge
Old Story Time
Over Our Way
Songs of Silence
Sprat Morrison
The Sun's Eye
The Wine of Astonishment
The Year in San Fernando
The Young Warriors

**For additional content and free resources head to
www.hoddereducation.com/caribbean-contemporary-classics**